OFF-OFF BROAD[

Thirty-[

Selected by New York theatre critics, professionals, and the editorial staff of Samuel French, Inc. as the most important plays of the Thirty-First Off-Off Broadway Original Short Play Festival sponsored by Love Creek Productions.

LE SUPERMARCHÉ
by Ian August

LIBRETTO
by Robin Rothstein

PLAY #3
by Harley Adams

SICK
by Bekah Brunstetter

PISCHER
by Ted Nusbaum

RELATIONTRIP
by Sharyn Rothstein

SAMUEL FRENCH, INC.

45 West 25th Street
NEW YORK 10010
LONDON

7623 Sunset Boulevard
HOLLYWOOD 90046
TORONTO

IMPORTANT BILLING AND CREDIT REQUIREMENTS

All producers of of *LE SUPERMARCHÉ, LIBRETTO, PLAY #3, SICK, PISCHER,* and *RELATIONTRIP must* give credit to the Author (s) of the Play(s) in all programs distributed in connection with performances of the Play(s) and in all instances in which the titles of the Play(s) appear for purposes of advertising, publicizing or otherwise exploiting the Play(s) and/or a production. The name of the Author(s) *must* also appear on a separate line, on which no other name appears, immediately following the Title(s), and *must* appear in size of type not less than fifty percent the size of the Title type.

TABLE OF CONTENTS

LE SUPERMARCHÉ
Or What I Did for Lunch

A One-Course Meal by

Ian August

LE SUPERMARCHÉ was produced for the Samuel French Off-Off Broadway Short Play Festival by PoffyBoo Productions, June 2, 2006. It was directed by Ken Wiesinger and stage managed by Keara Hailey Gordon. The cast was as follows:

The GIRL	Lea Eckert
The BOY	Eben Gordon
The NARRATOR	Ian August

LE SUPERMARCHÉ was originally produced by the New Jersey Repertory Company, 179 Broadway, Long Branch, NJ—Theatre Brut Festival, March 6, 2005. Artistic Director, SuzAnne Barabas; Executive Producer, Gabor Barabas. It was directed by Jim Donovan. The cast was as follows.

The GIRL	Lea Eckert
The BOY	Eben Gordon
The NARRATOR	Ames Adamson

Special thanks to Matthew Campbell,
and to Barbara and Jim August, on whom this twisted story
of love, food and poison was based.

CHARACTERS

The NARRATOR: a Narrator
The GIRL: a Girl
The BOY: a Boy

SETTING

Somewhere that is not France.

TIME

Sometime that is not too long ago.

(The set is that of a kitchen interior. One nonmoving countertop with stove lies stage center. Behind the counter rests kitchen cabinets, from which the actors will remove props and scene pieces. There is a refrigerator facade beside the cabinets, from which the BOY will make all entrances and exits. The countertop acts as an all-purpose set piece, for chairs, the bed, stove, etc.

Lights up on the NARRATOR stage center. Behind him on either side, frozen in athletic tableau, are the BOY, in chef's hat, and the GIRL, in apron. As he speaks, they come to life.)

NARRATOR. "Le Supermarche" or "What I Did for Lunch." The Characters: The Girl—

GIRL. A Girl.

NARRATOR. The Boy—

BOY. A Boy.

NARRATOR. The Setting: Somewhere that is not France. The Time: Sometime that is not too long ago. *(Beat)* It starts with a Girl.

GIRL. Hello.

NARRATOR. And then adds a boy.

BOY. How ya doin?

NARRATOR. Basic recipes require basic ingredients. *(To GIRL)* On the one side: chewy, slender, sinuous; perfect for stocks and sauces. Bring the pot to a boil; add carrots, celery, fennel, two small red onions and a three-inch-long piece of ginger root.

GIRL. I adore ginger root.

NARRATOR. Salt and Pepper to taste. For the more adventurous palate, try a little sweet basil for that something extra.

GIRL. I used to have a smoky flavor, but then I tried the patch.

NARRATOR. *(To BOY)* And on the other side: bold, broad, hefty and savory—whether the heart of the stew or the filling of the crepe. Juicy, bloody and tenderized barely within the boundaries of decency—nearly falling off the bone.

7

BOY. I'm leaner than I used to be.

NARRATOR. And we love you all the more for it.

GIRL. I know I do.

NARRATOR They meet in le supermarché.

BOY. We're French?

NARRATOR. Le supermarché, where silver-wrapped confections play hide-and-seek behind picket fenced registers; where clean-ups abound in aisle five, home of boxed soups, salad dressings, cooking oils and condiments of assorted viscous quality; where swift bursts of spray make tiered produce glisten in the halo of fluorescent light above.

BOY and GIRL. It's beautiful.

NARRATOR. It starts. Reaching for the same bruised head of radicchio.

BOY. I'm sorry … my fault.

GIRL. No, it's mine.

NARRATOR. There is an instantaneous connection.

BOY. I've seen you here before.

GIRL. I've been here many times.

BOY. So have I.

GIRL. You have? *(Pause)* I'm twenty-three years old and I don't expect to live past thirty. I recently moved out of my parent's house into a really cozy studio uptown where the landlady calls me "hon" and my next door neighbor has three cats named Blinky, Slinky, and Melba. I'm a Sagittarius and passionate about my art and my work and my family and my manicures. Do these avocadoes look ripe to you? You can stop me any time and tell me that you love me.

BOY. And I do.

NARRATOR. And they do. A whirlwind romance, coupled with a burning infatuation for all things delicious. Observe:

GIRL. Tell me how you love me.

BOY. I love you the way custard grows in beige flowers on a bed of lime gelato.

GIRL. Yes?

BOY. I love you the way crystal shimmers in the light bouncing through shitake consommé.

GIRL. Yes?

BOY. I love you the way Jarlsburg Swiss lays languorous over a *hot-heavy-open-faced Reuben.*

(Pause)

GIRL. You have a lovely way with words.

(They kiss hungrily.)

NARRATOR. The scene is stirred, and liberally sweetened with Splenda. And as the watched pot comes to a boil, the girl and the boy are married. They move to a little house in the country where he garnishes her with gourmet gifts and she services him with succulent snackings. But like all vegetables who sit in the sun too long, the girl begins to wilt beneath the brilliant light of his love.

(BOY leaves into fridge.)

GIRL. At night I cry with tears that are salty like beef jerky. I love my husband, I love his touch and his taste, but I miss the pleasures of my youth: my simple past, my studio apartment and the landlady who called me "hon," and Blinky and Slinky and Melba. I miss my art and my work and my family and my manicures. And how can I possibly die at age thirty?

(He enters from fridge.)

BOY. Syrup, I'm home. How was your morning?
GIRL. Bland.
BOY And your afternoon?
GIRL. Tepid.
BOY. I sent you flowers at lunch—did you get them?
GIRL. I ate them.
BOY. Walnut, what's going on? We were so happy before. What can I do to make your pain evaporate? My heart is heavy with cream.
NARRATOR. She does not answer, for what can she say? So she

stews.

GIRL. I simmer.

NARRATOR. She blanches.

GIRL. I boil.

NARRATOR. She fries.

GIRL. I bake.

NARRATOR. It's healthier. Remove from the oven at 350 degrees and poke the top with a toothpick. If it's done, the toothpick will emerge clean as a whistle.

(The BOY pokes her with a toothpick; she turns on him.)

GIRL. (*Angrily*) It's clean. I'm done.

(BOY exits into fridge.)

NARRATOR. So she returns to the place of her comfort, the place of her peace, the place where walls are lined with brightly colored cans of beans and aisles arc draped with banners saying "Buy, Buy!" and "50 Cents Off Two Bags of Muffins!"

GIRL. Le supermarche.

NARRATOR. And it is here, wandering among the frozen fish patties, where she meets ... the Shrink-Wrapped Man.

(The NARRATOR becomes the SHRINK-WRAPPED MAN.)

GIRL. Who…. Who are you?

SHRINK-WRAPPED MAN.

I come when saline stains the tiles

To offer aid and send for smiles

For when the kugel hits the fan

They call for me—the Shrink-Wrapped Man.

GIRL. You speak in couplets.

SHRINK-WRAPPED MAN.

Why so glum, my little peach?

With happiness so near your reach?

GIRL. Do I have to respond in couplets?

SHRINK-WRAPPED MAN.
Allow me to endear myself
Before I jump back on the shelf
I sense in you a great unrest
That lays beneath your turkey breast.

GIRL. You're right. You're strange, but you're right. I'm flustered. I'm frustrated. I feel eclaired and ignored. I hate my life, and I hate our little house, and I'm so furious with my husband I could scream—

SHRINK-WRAPPED MAN.
But ere you share your noise pollution
I have for you a quick solution:

(The SHRINK-WRAPPED MAN hands her a package.)

GIRL. What the hell is this?
SHRINK-WRAPPED MAN.
Within this packet you desire
Resides ingredients of fire
Create concoctions piping hot
A sumptuous stew to hit the spot
Just sprinkle chili with this spice—
I'm sure your spouse will not think twice
For even with one tiny taste,
Your sour will turn sweet—post-haste!

GIRL. Wait, I'm confused. My life will improve if I feed this to my hubby?
SHRINK-WRAPPED MAN.
Just take my missive by the letter
And what was vile will taste much better!

GIRL. You're very impressive. You should write a book.

(The SHRINK-WRAPPED MAN becomes the NARRATOR.)

NARRATOR. And with that, the Shrink-Wrapped Man was gone.

GIRL. Where'd he go?

(BOY re-enters from the fridge; he and GIRL lie in "bed.")

NARRATOR. That night, beneath a crescent moon—

BOY. *(Correcting him)* Croissant moon. We're French, remember?

NARRATOR. … While her husband slept, his wife lay beside him—like salad, tossing, and like rotisserie chicken, turning—the words of the Shrink-Wrapped Man echoing in her head. And when the cinnamon morning rolled around she had slept barely a wink.

BOY. Baby Greens, you're so tired. I can see it in your eyes.

GIRL. *(Curtly)* I think it's something I ate.

BOY. Why don't I come home early today? We'll have lunch and spend the rest of the day loafing together. Does that sound nice? Sweet potato? Ratatouille?

GIRL. I'll make lunch. A chili. Meaty and strong and spicy.

BOY. Sounds amazing. I'll be home at noon.

(He kisses her on the check, exits. The GIRL grabs a pan from a cabinet.)

NARRATOR. In a medium-sized saucepan she warms over the stove, her oil begins to sizzle, her garlic begins to pop. And the morning passes as molasses.

GIRL. Nine Thirty. Ten Seventeen. Eleven O'clock.

NARRATOR. *(With sinister glee)* And now, placing herself over high heat, the Girl begins to mix the mysterious chili. In a Calphalon Commercial Nonstick 10-inch Everyday Pan with Lid, she adds: one pound ground beef; one can kidney beans, drained; half of a Vidalia onion and half of a green bell pepper, seeded, stemmed, washed and chilled. Then she reaches for the packet from the strange old man.

GIRL. After all, revenge is a dish best served with dried pepper flakes.

NARRATOR. And it starts.

GIRL. *(A la al the witches of Macbeth)*
This bag of spice to do the chore
Ingredients with heat galore:
A bit of chili powder here,

A tiny drop of Worcestershire,
And in the pot that he's consumin'
A modest healthy dose of cumin
A Jalapeno, mustard seed
And horseradish to suit the need
One habanera, hint of sage,
Two parts Tabasco—one part RAGE!

(There is an explosion from her pan.)

BOY. *(Re-entering from the refrigerator with a bouquet of broccoli)* Salomon, I bought these for you.
GIRL. Put them in the crisper with the others. You hungry?
BOY. Famished! Mmm. It smells incredible!
GIRL. Have some. *(She dishes him some chili.)* Bon appetite!
BOY. *(Turning to an audience member, aside)* We're French.

(The BOY looks up at the GIRL, grabs a spoon, and takes a mouthful of the chili. His eyes open widely.)

NARRATOR. The girl looks on anxiously as the boy takes a spoonful of the mixture. She can see the tears welling in his eyes; his face becomes lobster red; she can feel the heat radiating from his body. And she thinks:
GIRL. This is it! He'll finally understand my unhappiness! The chili must be totally INEDIBLE.
NARRATOR. But the boy simply looks at her and smiles.
BOY. *(With some difficulty.)* It's delicious.
NARRATOR. And with sweat streaming down his tomato face, he takes another bite.
GIRL. What?
NARRATOR. And another.
GIRL. No—
NARRATOR. And another.
GIRL. Stop.
NARRATOR. But he does not stop. The Girl stands helpless as bite after bite, spoonful after spoonful, the chili in front of her hus-

band begins to disappear. In pain, impassioned and determined, the Boy licks the Corningware clean.

GIRL. He can't—

NARRATOR. But he did. Look.

GIRL. *(To the BOY)* But why, Corn Chip? Why would you keep eating?

NARRATOR. The Boy opened his mouth, but no words could come. For having consumed the entire bowl of chili, it had rendered him unable to speak. And more terrible yet—it had left him completely bereft of the ability to taste.

GIRL. What were you thinking?

NARRATIVE. And looking up into her eyes, the Boy wished that he could tell her—wished that the could share with her—

BOY. *(To NARRATOR.)* Uh, excuse me—d'you mind if I take this one?

NARRATOR. Not al all. Looking up into her eyes, but unable to speak, the Boy delivers a silent monologue:

BOY. *(To GIRL.)* Oh, Sno-cone, I know you're unhappy. I know you've given up everything to be with me. And with every red-hot bite I could feel your anger, I could taste your pain. But I couldn't stop. I had to go on. Because you made it for me. You chopped for me, you diced for me, you simmered for me and you spiced for me. And underneath that volcanic rage is a love that I know still warms your heart, as your chili warms my stomach. Within that chili was the heart of you. I've lost my ability to speak and I've lost my ability to taste, but I will never lose my ability to love you.

GIRL. Oh, that's beautiful.

BOY. I wish you could have heard it.

GIRL. Me, too.

(There is a pause, and the GIRL goes to the pan.)

NARRATOR. And before you can say "Blackened Scrod with Bok Choy Wrapped Couscous and Grilled Eggplant Sandwiches," the Girl takes up the spoon and begins eating the remains of the poisonous chili, right out of the pan! Her eyes burn and her hair sizzles, and when she is done, she, too, is left without speech, without taste, but with a fire burning in her heart hotter than it ever had before.

GIRL. Don't I get a monologue?

NARRATOR. No. In their anguish, in their passion, the Boy and Girl find a true love once more: a love greater than a fifty-pound bag of potatoes, a love stronger than a well-aged slab of gorgonzola, a love gentler than the aroma from a freshly snipped sprig of dill. A love not unlike the most scrumptious concoctions; before the recipe can be perfected, tidbits have to burn, temperatures regulated, condiments adjusted. Isn't that the way of all great meals?

(BOY and GIRL nod vigorously, turn to each other, and freeze in an athletic tableau.)

NARRATOR. And together they lived for the rest of their days, happily united by a mute but mutual understanding of one another, a newly developed appreciation for texture, and the praline and cream memory of their first culinary encounter—over a bruised head of radicchio—in Le Supermarché.

Fin

COSTUME PLOT

BOY
Red t-shirt
Blue jeans
White apron
White chef's hat
Sneakers
Clean socks of indeterminate color

GIRL
Blue t-shirt
Blue jeans
White apron
White chef's hat
Sneakers
Clean socks of indeterminate color

NARRATOR
Black suit
Long sleeve button-down yellow shirt
Black bow tie
Black dress shoes
Knee socks with frolicking kittens

SET PLOT

Countertop and range: stage center
Pot and pan rack: upstage right
Hollowed out refrigerator: upstage left
Two wooden stools: downstage of countertop

PROPERTY PLOT

PRESET
Three pots of various sizes" hanging from rack
Wooden spoon: set beneath counter

Additional chili ingredients: set beneath counter
Deck of cards: set atop refrigerator

<u>CARRIED ONSTAGE</u>
Grocery baskets (Boy and Girl)
Spice packet (Shrink Wrapped Man)
Head of broccoli (Boy)

SET DRAWING

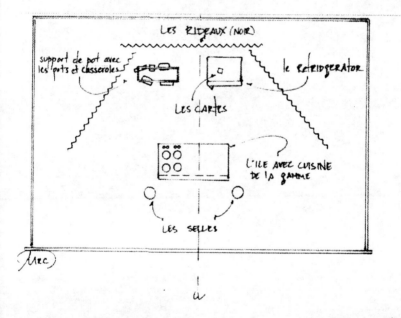

LIBRETTO

by

Robin Rothstein

LIBRETTO was presented in New York City by Algonquin Productions, Tony Sportiello, Artistic Director, in June 2006 as part of the Thirty-First Annual Off-Off Broadway Original Short Play Festival. The play was directed by Thomas Coté. The cast was as follows:

DOUGLAS	David M. Pincus
CLAIRE	Cailin McDonald

ABOUT THE AUTHOR

Robin Rothstein is the author of the original children's musical, *The Game Boy*, which received its world premiere at Vital Theatre Company. Her plays and monologues have been performed in New York City as well as across the country, and can be found in various collections. Several of her short plays have been finalists for the Heideman Award, including *In a Manner of Speaking*, which was produced at Actors Theatre of Louisville and published by Smith & Kraus. She is a member of The Dramatists Guild and Actors' Equity Association, and a graduate of the University of Pennsylvania.

CHARACTERS

CLAIRE
DOUGLAS

(Note: The characters may range anywhere from late 20's to early 50's, but both characters should appear to be about the same age. There should never be more than a ten-year difference between them.)

SETTING

The Metropolitan Opera

TIME

The present

20

(Sounds of an orchestra warming up. Sounds fade as lights rise on three theater seats. DOUGLAS sits in the stage left chair reading a program. The center chair has a coat folded on the seat. CLAIRE enters from stage left holding a ticket and a program. She looks at her ticket, then at DOUGLAS.)

CLAIRE. Excuse me.
DOUGLAS. Sure.

(DOUGLAS rises. CLAIRE makes her way to the third seat. She takes off her coat, puts it on her chair and sits on it. Once settled, she takes in more fully the splendor of her surroundings. After several moments, she looks at DOUGLAS and considers speaking to him. DOUGLAS feels CLAIRE looking at him. He looks up at her from his program.)

CLAIRE. Hello.
DOUGLAS. Hello.
CLAIRE. You come to the opera often?
DOUGLAS. I'm a subscriber.
CLAIRE. Ah. *(DOUGLAS looks back down at his program. Pause)* So. I guess you like it then.
DOUGLAS. *(Looking up)* Hm?
CLAIRE. You like the opera then.
DOUGLAS. Uh, yes.
CLAIRE. This is my first time. Guess you could call me a virgin. *(Chuckles)* I feel all tingly. This is very exciting. Do you feel tingly?
DOUGLAS. Uhhh...
CLAIRE. This is a pretty new experience for me. I'm not much of a culture vulture. Unless you consider going to a Rangers game culture. That's usually where I end up with my husband. He's got season tickets right down front so he can be real close to the fights.

21

Nice suit.

DOUGLAS. Uh … thank you.

CLAIRE. It's nice to dress up once in a while. I don't dress up like this so often. Usually just wear sweats to the Rangers games. Ricky, that's my husband, he always wants me to wear something nicer. He says I look too much like a slob when we go to the games, but I mean it's so freezing in there and people are spilling beer and popcorn all over. I mean, it's a hockey game, you know? What's the point, right?

DOUGLAS. Right.

(They smile at each other. There is nothing left to say. DOUGLAS looks back at his program.)

CLAIRE. *(Pause)* I bought this dress special for tonight. You like it?

DOUGLAS. *(Looking up)* It's, uh—it's very nice.

CLAIRE. Ricky said I looked silly in it and that it was a waste of money. It's a Donna Karan. *(Chuckles)* Actually it's a copy. I could never afford the real thing, but I think it looks just like the real thing, right? Don't you think? I think her stuff is really fabulous. That's a pretty splashy tie you got there.

DOUGLAS. Thank you.

CLAIRE. You pick that out yourself?

DOUGLAS. It was a present from someone.

CLAIRE. Your girlfriend.

DOUGLAS. Yes.

(He tries to return to reading his program)

CLAIRE. I knew it! I guess that's her coat then.

DOUGLAS. I beg your pardon?

CLAIRE. I was just saying this must be your girlfriend's coat then.

DOUGLAS. Oh, uh no. That's my coat.

CLAIRE. Oh. *(Pause)* Is she here yet?

DOUGLAS. *(Looking up)* Excuse me?

CLAIRE. I was just wondering if your girlfriend was here yet because the opera's gonna start like any minute—

DOUGLAS. She isn't coming this evening.

(DOUGLAS returns to his program.)

CLAIRE. Oh that's too bad. She sick or something?

DOUGLAS. No. She's fine.

CLAIRE. Oh, well that's good. 'Cause health is the most important thing. You have your health, you have everything. So why isn't she coming? Someone in her family sick?

DOUGLAS. No.

CLAIRE. I hope she didn't get stuck at work. That would be—

DOUGLAS. No, no. Nothing like that.

CLAIRE. *(Pause)* Traffic problems!

DOUGLAS. What…

CLAIRE. I never drive in the city for that very reason. I always take the railroad. So she get stuck in traffic?

DOUGLAS. No—!

CLAIRE. She needed to go out of town on business.

DOUGLAS. Look, she broke up with me today, okay! That's why she isn't here!

(DOUGLAS realizes he just made a small scene. He looks over his shoulder at the patrons behind him. He feels a sense of embarrassment and shame as lights go down to a ghost level and the song Questa o Quella *from ACT ONE of the opera* Rigoletto *begins. After ten or fifteen seconds, the music fades and lights rise fully on DOUGLAS sitting alone, absorbed in his program. His coat is still in the middle chair. CLAIRE approaches the aisle. DOUGLAS stands up and steps out of the aisle so she can enter.)*

CLAIRE. Jeez Louise! By the time I finished in the bathroom, the line was almost out to the stage. Good thing I got out quick! That's one thing I have to say about those Rangers games. Never have to wait on line for the little girls' room. You men got it easy no matter where you go though. In, out. Bim, bam, boom. *(She holds out her hand.)* I'm Claire by the way.

DOUGLAS. Douglas. *(They shake hands.)* Listen um … about before when I yelled at you like that, that was totally out of character—

CLAIRE. Eh, don't sweat it Doug, no biggy.

DOUGLAS. No, I, I don't ever express my emotions like that. Especially with a perfect stranger.

CLAIRE. Well, I mean, a break-up is a very emotional thing, Doug. It's important to express those kinds of emotions, otherwise … well … it just ain't healthy to keep the anger all bottled up inside.

DOUGLAS. That's true, but still—

CLAIRE. And I am the *perfect* perfect stranger 'cause I understand that first hand. So don't worry about it, okay? *Okay?*

DOUGLAS. Okay. Thank you. *(Pause)* So. Are you enjoying the opera?

CLAIRE. Um … yeah. Yeah. It's … very … you know … dense. Lots of stuff going on. And the sets are sooooo … wow. And the voices … when they sing real high, it makes me all teary. It's so beautiful.

DOUGLAS. Are you able to uh, you know, follow what's going on?

CLAIRE. Um … I must admit not really. What about you?

DOUGLAS. Well, I was an Italian minor, so…

CLAIRE. Wowwwwww. You worked in Italy as a miner? I never woulda got that from lookin' at you—

DOUGLAS. No, no, no. I minored in Italian. In college…

CLAIRE. Oh. Duhhhhh. Guess you can tell who *didn't* go to college. Probably the only one in this whole theater with just a high school education.

DOUGLAS. Oh, believe me, college isn't all it's cracked up to be. It's mostly four years of useless information followed by a lifetime of debt, so—

CLAIRE. But you learned Italian. That wasn't useless.

DOUGLAS. *(Smiles)* True.

CLAIRE. *(Pause)* You know. It's weird. I'm not sure·why … but even though I don't have a freakin' clue what any of these people are actually saying … I still … *know* what they're *saying?* That probably doesn't make any sense.

DOUGLAS. It makes complete sense.

(There is a short silence.)

CLAIRE. So … what happened?

DOUGLAS. Well, let's see. Rigoletto, the main character, has this daughter who—

CLAIRE. No. I mean with your girlfriend. Why'd she break up with you?

DOUGLAS. Oh. I uh … it's … it's rather complicated. I'd rather not—

CLAIRE. I'm sorry.

DOUGLAS. No, no—

CLAIRE. I'm prying—

DOUGLAS. It's okay—

CLAIRE. It's just that you seem like such a great guy. I can't understand who would want to let you go.

DOUGLAS. Thank you.

CLAIRE. *(Pause)* So you were beginning to explain … Rigoletto has this daughter…

DOUGLAS. Oh right, um, Gilda. *(Note: pronounced JEEL-da)* We find out at the beginning that the Duke falls in love with her—

CLAIRE. Okay…

DOUGLAS. But the Duke doesn't realize she's Rigoletto's daughter until he overhears Rigoletto telling Gilda's nurse to keep Gilda away from the corruption of the palace.

CLAIRE. Uh-huh…

DOUGLAS. After the Duke finds out all this…

CLAIRE. Uh-huh…

DOUGLAS. … he bribes the nurse to stay out of the way.

CLAIRE. Okay…

DOUGLAS. Now, at this point, the Duke decides he doesn't want to reveal his true identity…

CLAIRE. How come?

DOUGLAS. Well, he wants to get close to her, and he's a Duke and she's, you know, just a girl, a commoner, so he disguises himself as a student and they end up falling in love.

CLAIRE. I see. Okay, But then why did the Duke split so fast like that if he's so in love with her?

DOUGLAS. Well, people he knew were coming and he didn't want—

CLAIRE and DOUGLAS. —them to ruin his disguise.

DOUGLAS. There, see, you got it.

CLAIRE. Yeah?

DOUGLAS. Absolutely! You know much more than you think you do.

CLAIRE. Not really.

DOUGLAS. Sure you do. You're still able to get the sense of the libretto even though you don't understand what they're saying.

CLAIRE. What's that?

DOUGLAS. What.

CLAIRE. The libretto? What is that?

DOUGLAS. Oh. Well. The libretto is the story of the opera. It's the book. The plot. But really, the libretto is just words. It's what's going on beneath the libretto, the emotional truth of the characters … their desires … that's the real story. It's like you were saying before, it's not so much what they're saying, it's … you were moved. This opera touches you someplace.

CLAIRE. Yeah.

(CLAIRE looks down at her program. DOUGLAS gently touches CLAIRE's arm.)

DOUGLAS. Hey…

(CLAIRE jerks away.)

CLAIRE. What!

DOUGLAS. Oh. I'm—

CLAIRE. I…

DOUGLAS. I'm sorry—I—

CLAIRE. No, I'm sorry.

DOUGLAS. I didn't mean to scare you—
CLAIRE. No I—
DOUGLAS. I just—
CLAIRE. I don't know why I jumped like that.
DOUGLAS. I just thought you might … prefer putting your coat here with mine … instead of, you know, sitting on it…
CLAIRE. Oh…
DOUGLAS. You might be more comfortable.
CLAIRE. Um … sure, sure. Yeah. That would be good. *(CLAIRE rises. She picks up her coat and is about to put it on the middle chair, but DOUGLAS takes the coat from her. He shakes her coat out, neatly folds it and then carefully lays it on top of his. He sits.)* Thanks.
DOUGLAS. Sure.

(After a few moments, lights dim to a ghost level. Parmi veder le la-grime *plays for ten to fifteen seconds, representing ACT TWO of the opera. In the ghost light, DOUGLAS moves the coats from the middle chair to the chair he was sitting in and he moves to sit in the middle seat, next to CLAIRE. The music fades and lights rise fully again.)*

CLAIRE. So the Duke knows!
DOUGLAS. And, right, and so he goes to find her.
CLAIRE. And Rigoletto has no clue.
DOUGLAS. No, not at all.
CLAIRE. Now what about when all those guys came back?
DOUGLAS. Which guys?
CLAIRE. The ones who took Gilda.
DOUGLAS. Oh, well, they think Gilda's Rigoletto's mistress.
CLAIRE. Rigoletto's mistress?
DOUGLAS. Yeah, they don't know she's his daughter! So, when he's upset that Gilda's missing, they don't understand why he's that upset.
CLAIRE. Why doesn't he tell them she's his daughter?
DOUGLAS. He does.
CLAIRE. He does?
DOUGLAS. After he realizes that Gilda is with the Duke he tells

them she's his daughter.

CLAIRE. Oh. Now—okay—she goes back to her father right?

DOUGLAS. Yes. *But* she tells Rigoletto that she's in love with the Duke, but she doesn't realize he's the Duke.

CLAIRE. Wait wait wait. She *still* doesn't know the Duke's a Duke?

DOUGLAS. No, she still thinks he's a student.

CLAIRE. Rigoletto looked pretty pissed off there at the end of Act Two. I bet he's gonna kick someone's butt in Act Three, right? *(DOUGLAS laughs.)* What. What's so funny?

DOUGLAS. Nothing…

CLAIRE. What. Come on.

DOUGLAS. It's just … you have a very honest way of speaking.

(CLAIRE looks away, somewhat hurt.)

CLAIRE. I'm sorry…

DOUGLAS. Oh. No, no. It's nice.

CLAIRE. *(Pause. Smiles)* Thanks.

(Lights remain up as we hear the final thirty seconds or so of Chi è mai, chi è qui in sua vece? *As the music plays, DOUGLAS and CLAIRE simultaneously and unconsciously take each other's hand. CLAIRE is completely absorbed and moved by these final moments of the opera. The song reaches its conclusion. The opera is over.*

DOUGLAS and CLAIRE applaud. CLAIRE is on the brink of tears, or it's possible the dam may even have broke, and she begins to cry. When they finish applauding there is a brief silence.)

DOUGLAS. So. What uh … what made you decide to buy a ticket to this opera?

CLAIRE. I didn't buy it actually.

DOUGLAS. Oh.

CLAIRE. I won it at a charity raffle.

DOUGLAS. Oh really?

CLAIRE. Yeah.

DOUGLAS. Well that's nice.

CLAIRE. Yeah.

DOUGLAS. What was the charity raising money for?

CLAIRE. Victims of domestic violence. You know, it's funny, I almost gave the ticket away, but I figured, what the hell, ya know? It'll be a new experience.

DOUGLAS. *(Pause)* Claire? Would you get a coffee with me?

CLAIRE. *(Pause)* Oh.

DOUGLAS. There's this wonderful, cozy café nearby—

CLAIRE. I … I don't know. *(She looks at her watch)* I don't think … I should. Ricky might start to worry.

DOUGLAS. Just a quick cappuccino.

(DOUGLAS gently puts his hand on CLAIRE's knee.)

CLAIRE. *(Pause)* I can't. I want to. But I can't.

(DOUGLAS takes CLAIRE's hand.)

DOUGLAS. Please … I'm enjoying this Claire. Aren't you?

(CLAIRE looks at him. She is torn and filled with emotion. After several moments, she removes her hand and looks out.)

CLAIRE. It was really, really nice meeting you Doug.

DOUGLAS. *(Pause)* It was really, really nice meeting you too Claire. *(DOUGLAS rises and takes his coat.)* Take care of yourself.

CLAIRE. You too.

(DOUGLAS starts to exit, then stops. He is upstage left with his back to the audience as he fumbles for a pen in his jacket pocket. When he finds it, he writes on something then walks back to the aisle.)

DOUGLAS. Claire? *(CLAIRE looks at him.)* Um, this is a season brochure. *(He hands her a large thin booklet.)* If you, you know, ever want to come to the opera again … well … I put my number on the front, so, you know, you can call me. If you want.

*(CLAIRE tries to smile through her tears. DOUGLAS hesitates, then
    exits. CLAIRE looks at the brochure, then hugs it to her chest, as
    she begins to cry more fully.
Lights slowly fade to black.)*

End of play

COSTUMES

CLAIRE is dressed nicely enough, but one should get a sense by the color or flare of her dress that she is probably not very accustomed to attending upscale events. She should be carrying a pocketbook as well.

DOUGLAS is dressed conservatively in a suit or blazer. His tie should stand out a little.

CLAIRE and DOUGLAS both need to have a coat.

PROPERTIES

2 opera tickets
1 theater ticker
1 opera season brochure
1 pen
1 pocket-sized pack of tissues for Claire (optional) or 1 handkerchief
    for Douglas (optional)

SET DESCRIPTION

3 identical chairs representing part of a row of theater seats

PLAY #3

by

Harley Adams

Scene 1

(A hallway. PETE is unlocking his door. JOHN walks on.)

JOHN. Hey, are you new here?

PETE. Oh, yes, hi. We just moved in.

JOHN. Well it's nice to meet you. I'm John. I live here … in 9G.

PETE. Well we just moved in to 9F.

JOHN. Who's the "we"?

PETE. Sorry, I'm Pete. My wife is Camilla. And we have a daughter, Maria. We're the Murphy's.

JOHN. The Murphy's. Not related to Eddie Murphy I presume.

PETE. No.

JOHN. *(Laughs)* Yeah, I didn't think so. That would be a bit weird, right? Because you're not black. I would have to ask some questions then, right?

PETE. *(Dry laugh)* Yeah I guess so.

JOHN. So how long you been married?

PETE. About four years now.

JOHN. Oh I see. Has it started to suck yet? Have you reached the point where you hate each other?

PETE. *(Dry laugh)* No. No not yet.

JOHN. Yeah well you just wait until you stop having sex.

PETE. *(Dry laugh)* Right. Are you married?

JOHN. Oh, haha, no. I just watch a lot of those … you know … those fucking marriage sitcoms. So I guess I just feel like I know all about it from TV.

PETE. Right well it's very different.

JOHN. Yeah I guess. But you just wait until you stop having sex and then you tell me if it's different

PETE. Haha, alright I will.

JOHN. In fact, come tell me as soon as you stop having sex, and then I'll come knocking on your door, "Oh Mrs. Murphy? Mrs. Mur-

phy? I hear your having some marital troubles ... can I come in?"
Haha, right?

PETE. *(Dry laugh)* Right. Well it's good to know you've ... uh
... got my back.

JOHN. Haha, yeah. Well I'm just fucking with you anyways. I
don't even know your wife. What's your daughter's name?

PETE. Maria. She's three.

JOHN. Ah, that's a good age. Too young to be causing any trou-
ble. You just wait.... I've seen it on TV. *(Laughs)*

PETE. Oh, well, she's a good little girl.

JOHN. Yeah I'm sure. Must be very pretty. Pretty little name,
Maria.

PETE. Yes.

JOHN. *(Starts singing awkwardly)* "How do you solve a problem
like Maria?" *(Laughs)* Right? You know what that is?

PETE. Yeah that's the—

JOHN. It's the Sound of Music.

PETE. Yup.

JOHN. Nuns. *(There is an awkward pause.)* Well hey so listen, if
you ever feel like ... you know ... coming over for dinner ... or coming to watch some TV, just to shoot the breeze, or you wanna bring
the wife and kid, you know, just come over anytime. You don't even
have to call. I'm here all the time.

PETE. Oh well thanks that's very kind of you to offer. I think
we're just sort of settling in so...

JOHN. Oh and hey, if you bring the wife I promise I won't try
anything. I'll wear a bad shirt so I don't look so fucking handsome.

PETE. Right, thanks.

JOHN. Alright, I'll see you later.

PETE. Nice to meet you.

JOHN. Same here.

(They close their respective doors.)

Scene 2

(JOHN is in the hallway and PETE walks in.)

JOHN. Hey.

PETE. Oh hey.

JOHN. It's been a while, haven't seen you.

PETE. Yeah I guess so.

JOHN. How's your daughter? Maria, right?

PETE. Oh she's fine.

JOHN. Good, good. How old is she again?

PETE. Three.

JOHN. That's great. That is a great age.

PETE. Yup.

JOHN. You know, I've been meaning to tell you, I was on the street the other day, coming into the building like at night. And I usually look up to my window, even though I know no one's gonna be there, but just for kicks you know? But I looked next to my window to yours, and I could see, like clearly see, your TV. All the way from the street. Like all the way down on the street, I could see your TV. It's so fricken' big it's hilarious. I actually stood there for a minute just watching it. I guess cuz its projection you can see it so clearly. I mean, how much does that projection stuff cost?

PETE. Quite a bit.

JOHN. Yeah I bet. I mean I actually stood there for a full minute just mesmerized by the size ... by your *mother fucking* magnanimous screen. I think you were watching football. It was great.

PETE. Yeah it's pretty big.

JOHN. You bet your ass it's pretty big. But you know what they say ... I mean .... with the size of your TV and all ... I bet you have a pretty small penis. *(Pause)* Huh? *(Pause)* Am I right? I bet you do.

PETE. Hah. Umm.... I don't know.

JOHN. Well that's what they say.

PETE. Right.

JOHN. Yeah. Well it is pretty fucking big.

PETE. Uhuh.

JOHN. I don't mean your penis, haha, I mean your TV.

PETE. Right.

JOHN. I mean I don't know how big your penis is.

PETE. Right. *(Pause)* Well I should probably go in, my wife's waiting for me.

JOHN. Yeah, I bet, waiting for your small penis. Huh? You know if you really do have a small penis, in time, I think she'll look for … length outside the bedroom … if you know what I mean. And in that case, you better watch out, cuz I'm right next door, and I may not have a huge projection TV, but I do have a twelve-inch cock.

PETE. Oh.

JOHN. *(Laughs)* Haha, I'm just kidding ya pal. Twelve inches is a fucking monstrosity. I'm pretty big but I certainly don't have twelve inches. I don't even think they … well actually you know … some of those guys in porn … you know … some of those guys are pretty big. Like Peter North.

PETE. I … uh … I don't watch much porn.

JOHN. Yeah well he's done a lot of stuff, pretty famous. He's not twelve inches but he's pretty big I guess. Twelve inches is way out of control.

PETE. Right.

JOHN. A twelve-inch penis. G-d.

PETE. *(Pause)* Well I should probably get going … so….

JOHN. Right right sure, I guess I'll see you later. Or maybe I'll just watch you from the street.

PETE. Hah. Alright, have a nice night.

JOHN. You too.

Scene 3

PETE. Hey.

JOHN. Oh hey there.

PETE. You know I have to say thank you to you. My wife … she told me what you did, and I have to say thanks.

JOHN. Oh it's no problem.

PETE. My daughter was really ... she was ecstatic. She couldn't stop talking—

JOHN. Maria? Oh she—

PETE. Yeah she couldn't stop talking about the pancakes and how you ... she was very happy.

JOHN. Oh that's great. She is a great kid, she really ate those pancakes. I mean she swallowed them *whole*.

PETE. Well she really loved them, she couldn't stop talking about them.

JOHN. Is that so?

PETE. Yeah. She—

JOHN. Well that's great. It was no problem. No problem at all. You know I'll come over—I told your wife that I'd come over anytime to make gummy bear pancakes.

PETE. Oh well that's very kind of you. I am very intrigued as well ... I mean ... how do you get the gummy bears in there? I've never heard of that before.

JOHN. Oh it's an old family recipe. It's really quite simple ... you just gotta make the batter a certain way and then make sure the gummy bears stay in ... and they just sort of get cooked in with the pancake mix.

PETE. I see.

JOHN. They were my favorite when I was a kid, and I just love makin' em.

PETE. Well apparently they're delicious.

JOHN. Well you know, you're wife comes over, comes knockin' on my door, middle of the afternoon, asking for *milk*. She can't find the milk, she doesn't have any milk ... she doesn't want to run out to the store, she comes over here, comes knockin' on my door. She doesn't know me you know, but I got the milk, I always have milk. I told her, I told her I always have milk. So I bring it over, she tells me she's making pancakes. From scratch ... that's why she needs the milk ... for Maria. Maria wants pancakes, on some kind of whim, in the middle of the afternoon, and so she's making pancakes for her. Great mom. What a great mom.

PETE. Yes she is.

JOHN. My mom was like that. She taught me how to make the

gummy bear pancakes. So I say, you know, I see she's making pancakes, I say can I help, I know a recipe for gummy bear pancakes ... she laughs. She laughs at the idea of gummy bear pancakes. Everybody laughs at first, but then when you try them ... and they're not easy to make, you gotta make sure the gummy bears don't fall out of the batter, and that they don't melt into the pan ... but if they come out just right, man are they delicious.

PETE. Well my daughter certainly thought they were delicious.

JOHN. Yeah I bet ... she wolfed them down. Quite a stomach that girl's got.

PETE. Yeah.

JOHN. I bet it was the gummy bears though ... anything with candy ... kids just love....

PETE. Yeah she loves candy.

JOHN. And your wife loved the pancakes too. We all sat down and had gummy bear pancakes in the middle of the afternoon. It was great. On your lovely oak wood dining table. We had gummy bear pancakes. *(Laughs)*. Funny thing, isn't it?

PETE. *(Laughs)* Yeah. Well thanks. Thanks a lot. It was really great of you.

JOHN. It was no problem. No problem at all. I'd come over anytime and make gummy bear pancakes. Really.

PETE. Thanks.

JOHN. And I finally got to see your place. And I have to say, you have a beautiful family. I really admire you.

PETE. Thank you.

JOHN. No I am serious; I would kill for a family like that.

PETE. Well thanks.

JOHN. I mean you've got this beautiful little girl. And my g-d, your wife ... is gorgeous. I mean *gorgeous*. I got a chance to look at her while I was cooking, and I am speaking sincerely now, she has got it all going on. Two of the most amazing, full, supple looking *breasts* I have ever seen in my life. I am serious. That woman ... Camilla isn't it ... she has got some pair of tits. I mean those things are melons. *Melons*.

PETE. Ummm ... thanks.

JOHN. You're damn right you say thanks, I am giving you one of the best compliments you can get, "*You're wife has mind-blowing knockers.*" Take it when it comes man.

PETE. I guess it's just not something you usually—

JOHN. I mean, sure, I can make gummy bear pancakes, that's all well and great, but *you* ... your *wife* ... I mean.... *(Pause)* ...Are they real?

PETE. What?

JOHN. Are those things real?

PETE. Oh ... well ... umm ... I don't know if I quite feel *comfortable* ... ummm ... revealing that ... just talking about that. I don't think it's something you usually....

JOHN. Hey come on man, its just us guys ... you can tell me ... were just shootin' the breeze here.

PETE. I'm sorry but I just don't—

JOHN. Alright I see how it is. You're just letting me leave it up to the old imagination. So that when I'm up at night lying in bed I can wonder whether your wife's tits are real.

PETE. No, I—

JOHN. Well I guess it's better I don't know ... so thanks. But she is quite a looker. A 9.5 out of 10 my friend. And I don't usually give those ... so be grateful.

PETE. Right. Well you know I should probably get in, I—

JOHN. Oh yeah ... sure go on in. I'll see you later.

PETE. Right.

JOHN. But I'll see you're wife tonight. *In my mind. (Laughs)*.

PETE. Well that's good to know.

JOHN. Alright see you later. And hey, tell your family that any time they want gummy bear pancakes, just come knockin' on 9G.

PETE. I sure will. I'm sure they'll take you up on that.

JOHN. Good. Cuz I love makin' 'em.

PETE. Well alright ... see you later.

JOHN. Yup ... bye.

(They go to their respective doors.)

Scene 4

PETE. Hi.

JOHN. Oh Pete, hey, I uh, got one of your … the mailman must have put a letter of yours in my box.

PETE. Oh.

JOHN. So I have it in apartment.

PETE. Oh thanks.

JOHN. Yeah it was some friend of your daughters it seemed like, RSVP-ing to an invite to her birthday party, I believe.

PETE. You opened it?

JOHN. Oh, well yeah.

PETE. Why?

JOHN. I wanted to see if it was for me.

PETE. But didn't it say 9F on the cover?

JOHN. Yeah, but maybe the person marked it wrong. Maybe that was why it was in my box.

PETE. That doesn't make any sense.

JOHN. Well I just wanted to check. I mean….

PETE. Right well I guess I'd just appreciate if you—

JOHN. It was just a party RSVP. And speaking of party's, you didn't tell me your daughter was having a birthday party. I would love to come.

PETE. Oh, well it's really just only kids. I mean she is three. Turning four.

JOHN. Oh well I'm a big kid anyways. I'm just a big kid.

PETE. Right. Well it really is only kids, or else we would have invited you.

JOHN. And hey! I could make gummy bear pancakes for the party! Your daughter would love that!

PETE. Yeah I guess she would like that…

JOHN. She asked for them again the other day. I saw her in the lobby.

PETE. Oh yeah?

JOHN. Just standing there. So cute. Three years old. Wow. Almost four. She comes running up to me … dragging her mom along

… you know, like little kids do *(Doing an impression of a little kid)*
"Mommy, mommy, can you ask the man to make the gummy pancakes again? Please please please?" Camilla was so embarrassed. I
told her I'd come over anytime to make 'em. Anytime. Your daughter
got so excited. Her little dimples just …. g-d, she is so cute. Can I just
say … can I speak honestly for a second? She is…. When she grows
up … lots of guys are gonna want her. I mean … she is a looker. She
is actually … really hot. I mean … she is only three, but what I am
saying is that she has great potential. When she's older … man, she is
gonna be beautiful. Just like your wife. Lots of guys are gonna be
crawling after her. Hell, I *already* … well I mean she's only three.
Only four actually. Or is she still three? When is her birthday?

PETE. *(His attitude and tone has changed during this speech.)*
What?

JOHN. When is her—

PETE. What the hell is wrong with you? *(Getting madder and
madder)* What the—is there something wrong with you?

JOHN. Whaddayou mean?

PETE. To go talking about my *daughter* that way … she's only
three.

JOHN. Oh so she hasn't had her birthday—

PETE. She is just a child and you—are you some kind of *pedophile?* I mean, what the *fuck* is wrong with you? Huh? You can't just
talk about a person's child like that. It's … fucking Christ … you
can't do that. There is no way in hell you are coming to her party.

JOHN. Hey I was just—

PETE. I don't care. I don't care what you "were just." Your
whole thing … the way you step in here … the way you stand in this
hallway and talk about my *family*. The way you talk about my *wife*.
What the hell is wrong with you? How can you tell me those things?
You disgust me! You can't just talk like that about a guy's family!

JOHN. Hey man you're getting the wrong idea. I love your family…. I made them gummy bear pancakes! I told them anytime—

PETE. I don't care that you made them pancakes. I don't want
my daughter getting pancakes from a guy who … who thinks she's
hot! I don't want my *wife* near you! Because of you, you know what I
think about at night? I think about the fact that you are across the hall,

thinking about my wife! The sick things you would want to do … you sick pervert! And now you're thinking about my daughter too!? What are you? Some kind of sick pedophile?!

JOHN. No way…. I wasn't trying to—

(Suddenly, PETE grabs JOHN by the collar and pushes him by the neck up against the wall, holding him there while he talks right in his face. He is shaking with fury.)

PETE. I DON'T CARE WHAT YOU WERE TRYING TO DO! DO YOU HEAR ME!? I DON'T FUCKING CARE! ALL I CARE ABOUT IS YOU STAYING THE *FUCK* AWAY FROM MY FAMILY YOU DISGUSTING PERVERT PEDOPHILE SON OF A BITCH! DO YOU HEAR ME!? YOU FUCKING CUNT! YOU SICK CUNT! YOU ARE NOT TO THINK ABOUT, TALK ABOUT, OR SAY ANYTHING TO MY WIFE OR DAUGHTER EVER AGAIN! YOU LEAVE THEM ALONE, DO YOU HEAR ME!? YOU FUCKING PIECE OF SHIT!? IF MY WIFE COMES OVER TO YOUR DOOR, ASKING FOR MILK, YOU TELL HER YOU DON'T HAVE ANY, AND YOU CLOSE THE DOOR! DO YOU HEAR ME! YOU DON'T GIVE HER MILK, YOU DON'T MAKE PANCAKES! GOT THAT!? HUH!? WHAT ARE YOU GONNA DO IF MY WIFE COMES OVER!? HUH!? WHAT ARE YOU GONNA DO YOU FUCKING CUNT!?

JOHN. I … I … I'm…

PETE. ANSWER THE FUCKING QUESTION YOU PIECE OF SHIT! WHAT ARE YOU GONNA DO— *(Right then both men look to the side, where they see an old lady open her door--this is offstage and is taken off the two men's reactions—and after a moment PETE takes his hold off of JOHN as he talks to her.)* Oh … umm … hi Mrs. Bronfman. We're umm … we're just … discussing something … we're sorry … we're sorry for all the … we'll quiet down. We're fine. Sorry about that.

(She closes her door. PETE gives one last look at JOHN who is still standing nervously against the wall, and then turns to put his key in his door, leaving JOHN there. After a long awkward pause...)

JOHN. *(Very quiet and nervously, almost sheepishly)* Do you... uh ... do you ... still want that letter?

PETE. *(After a pause he responds abrasively and forcefully, but quietly.)* Just leave it under my door.

(He then exits through his door. JOHN stands for a bit in the hall, brushes himself off, and then unlocks and enters his door.)

Scene 5

(Lights up on PETE standing at John's door, he takes a breath for a moment before knocking. After a few moments the door opens.)

PETE. Hey.
JOHN. Hey.

(Pause)

PETE. Ok, look. About what happened ... I am *really* sorry. I ... I can't express how sorry I am. I was way out of line ... and I'm sorry that I ... well I shouldn't have gotten violent like that ... and well I really messed a lot of things up. I am extremely sorry. Is your neck alright?

JOHN. Oh yeah its fine, doesn't hurt at all.

PETE. Good. Well I'm sorry. And secondly, I wanted to *thank* you, for what you did for me. You really didn't have to do that and it meant a lot to me.

JOHN. What do you mean?

PETE. Well the building manager told me what you had said to her...and she said it was because of what you said that we weren't kicked out of the building. She apparently knows you very well.

JOHN. Who, Ms. Crutchfield? Oh yeah we've known each other a while.

PETE. Well what you told her really helped.... I mean if it wasn't for you Camilla and I wouldn't have this apartment right now.

JOHN. Well buddy, it was no problem.

PETE. I just, I feel awful … I mean after all you did … and *I*….

JOHN. Hey man … don't worry about it. Its fine. Its all in the past. We have got to move on. That's the only way to live your life … you gotta just get over things. Hell, I got over it, so you should to. I've forgotten it even happened.

PETE. Well thanks.

JOHN. I mean when I heard that Ms. Bronfman had *reported* you to the building manager … you know … and I've known her a long time but I was mad. I mean, who's she to go poking her nose around everywhere … sneaking around the hallways, reporting people to the building manager. She just needs to mind her own business. So I just went down to see Ms. Crutchfield, we go back a long ways, since I moved here, and I just told her, you know, that it was all a *misunderstanding*. That we were just messing around. I told her we were just having fun, playing around, being *guys* and that we were sorry that we made so much noise in the hallway. I told her that Ms. Bronfman got it all wrong, that we were just messing around. And it took some convincing, it took some talking, but she came around. She knows me really well.

PETE. Well thanks so much. You really didn't have to do that, and it meant a lot to me—

JOHN. *Of course* I had to do it. Of course. It was all a misunderstanding. I mean….we can't have Ms. Bronfman reporting us and spying on us like that…you know? She doesn't *understand* us. *(He starts to get chummy, lightly touching and slapping him on the arm.)* She doesn't understand us *guys*. She's an old lady. She's a *woman*. She doesn't understand how it works with men. How we *talk*. The *things*…it's a whole other world to her. *Women* don't understand men. They don't. They just don't get us. Our way of … way of … our way of being. Right?

PETE. Right.

JOHN. So I just had to go down to Ms. Crutchfield and straighten things out, no problem. And everything turned out fine, I mean, you get to stay. And everything's … everything with … with us, is … everything turned out *ok*.

PETE. Well once again thank you very much.

JOHN. It was no problem.

PETE. *(Pause)* Well listen … Camilla and I were wondering …. we thought that … would you like to come to Maria's birthday party this Saturday and make gummy bear pancakes for the kids?

JOHN. Would I like to come to her birthday party?

PETE. Yes. It's this sat—

JOHN. *(Excited)* I would love to come! Oh that's great! Thank you so much for inviting me. I'll make a huge batch of pancakes … how many … they'll all love 'em … how many kids are there? I can make a lot … they'll all love 'em. Kids just love gummy bear pancakes. Anything with sugar really, they just love. Me too. I love sugar. I'm just a big kid though. I'm just a big kid.

PETE. Well that's great. We'd love to have you. It's this Saturday at noon.

JOHN. *High Noon*! Excellent. Thanks so much for inviting me. You tell Camilla I said thank you.

PETE. *(He starts to head toward his door.)* I will … I'll tell her right now.

JOHN. Great. Great. Alright … thanks so much … and I'll see you Saturday at noon. With loads of gummy bear pancakes!

PETE. Sounds great.

(They both have their doors open now. Pause)

JOHN. And tell Maria that I'll be coming … she'll be so excited.

PETE. I will.

JOHN. Oh and Pete….

PETE. Yes?

JOHN. *(Joking)* I promise to keep it in my pants.

(After a moment JOHN closes his door, still smiling. PETE takes this in for a second, and then goes in his door.
Blackout)

The end

SICK

by

Bekah Brunstetter

CHARACTERS

B: 23, lady. Quieter counterpart
E: 23, lady. Loud, nearly inappropriate
humor, irresistible.

Kyle
Max
Paulo
Birthday Man
The Nurse
Two Sub-Nurses

ON TV
Samantha
Hot Guy
Hot Girl
Charlie
Condom Man

PLACE

A public health clinic in a large city, dirty part of tow.
The STD wing, waiting room.

TIME

Now.

STAGE

Rows or awkward, uncomfortable chairs.
Doors. Free Condoms. Literature.
A TV that drones constantly.

(B and E sit in the front row of in a large group of chairs in a waiting room. B holds a piece of paper reading numbered 19; E numbered 20. The TV drones. B is freaking out, slightly. E is bored. Both are girls in their early twenties. On the television, a woman, 30's and very 1988, speaks. The acting is, well, bad.)

WOMAN. Hi. My name is Samantha and I am *not* an actor. I am a real live seventeen-year-old girl. I am not a homosexual or a druggie. The fact that you're here is the first step. You should be proud of yourself. Getting tested is very, very brave. It's fear that perpetuates illnesses like AIDS.

My name is Samantha, and I am HIV positive. You're probably wondering why I am HIV positive. I don't look like I am HIV positive, do I? Well, I'm living with it, one step at a time. It was hard being a sixteen-year-old girl and finding out that I was HIV positive, being that I was only a sixteen-year-old girl at the time. Now, I am seventeen years old. It was Halloween. A Halloween party. I made a stupid mistake and snuck out the house to go to a party that I was interested in chilling at. I thought there would be some major babes there. There were. I thought it would be way cool. His name was Todd. He told me I was pretty. He told me he liked my sweater, which was purple.

(Slight tears.) I believed him.

He must have put something in my drink because I woke up in the bushes in the morning with no panties. I looked for my panties. I didn't know what to do. I walked home. Two months later, I found out I was HIV positive. I'll have to live with disease forever. I've done some things I am not proud of, but now, I can make up for my mistakes, by telling you my story.

It can happen to anyone. Can happen to anyone. *(The TV skips/is stuck.)* Can happen to anyone. Can happen to anyone. Can happen to anyone. Anyone. Anyone. Anyone.

(WOMAN freezes in a smile. Static from the television. A NURSE walks by and shakes it.

B and E, still waiting. E cannot contain her energy. Leaps up, grabs a handful of condoms from the table by the television. Puts them in her purse. Sits back down next to B.)

B. You're sick.

E. What? They're free.

B. I'm never having sex ever again.

E. Right.

B. No, I'm serious. I'm officially closed.

E. A little clammy-D never killed anybody.

B. SHHHH.

(Pause. E attempts to sit still but is way bored.

A NURSE, decked to the nines in faux gold, with a raunchy outfit in some animal print beneath her white lab coat, emerges with a clipboard. B and E perk up.)

NURSE. Letter G. Letter G. Letter G.

(No one responds. She goes off).

E. ... AIDS wouldn't be so bad. You'd night sweat off like thirty pounds. It'd be hot. And very poetic, that whole I'm slowly dying for my sins thing.

B. You're not helping.

E. You're not the first girl ever to get drunk on her birthday and accidentally fuck a short bald man without a condom.

B. He wasn't short.

(BIRTHDAY MAN appears behind them.)

BIRTHDAY MAN. I am not short. My whole life, people have called me short but I am above average, I am five foot seven and I fuck better than men half my age. *Twice* my age. I make sixty thousands dollars a year! My job has growth potential! I am currently up for promotion to Distribution! I fuck better than half my department! I've slept with ninety-seven women! My mom taught me how to make a nice marina sauce! I know the basics of sewing! But I'm still a man! I enjoy roller skating! I thought you were cute!

B. You never called.

BIRTHDAY MAN. I was—scared.

B. You don't even remember my name.

BIRTHDAY MAN. Elizabeth.

B. *(Motioning to E)* That's *her* name.

E. He sounds like a winner. *(B shrugs.)* I'm sure you're fine.

B. I don't know.

E. You'll get your results and forget all about it and before you know it you'll return to your usual loose self.

B. I'm not—I'm not *loose*.

E. Then what are you so worried about?

B. I don't know.

E. Did he, you know.

B. What?

E. Did he giz in your wad?

B. Oh, come on.

E. Did he?

BIRTHDAY MAN. I don't recall, uh. I don't recall—gizz-ing in your wad. I pulled out.

B. I don't remember. I was gone. I was asking hot dog vendors to go down on me. I could barely stand up.

E. Well, Happy Birthday.

B. I remember he had a fish, though. He had a fish tank and the fish was floating on the top.

E. It was dead?

B. Don't say dead.

(The NURSE comes out with a clipboard.)

NURSE. Letter Q? Letter Q? Letter Q? Letter Q?

(No one responds. The NURSE, unphased, exits.)

B. It's times like this I miss Max.

E. Max was lame. He ate your soul.

B. … He loved me. If I'd just stayed with him forever I'd never have to worry about shit like this. We could've had little bright-haired babies and lots of dogs.

E. You would've stuck your head in the oven before forever even got there. You were miserable.

B. It was comfortable, it was nice.

(MAX appears behind them.)

MAX. Did you fart?

B. *(Smiling)* No, Max. You did.

MAX. Yeah, you did, that fart smelled like you. It was definitely yours.

B. No I didn't.

MAX. Happy two-year anniversary.

B. Thanks.

MAX. We should make love.

B. Ha.

MAX. Why not?

B. Let's just go to sleep.

MAX. Okay.

B. I'll make you waffles in the morning.

MAX. Mmmm.

B. Rub my back?

MAX. Okay.

B. I got you those underwears's. Last April.

MAX. No you didn't.

B. Yeah I did.

MAX. No, my mom got them.

B. No, I did, I got them at Old Navy, they were $4.99 and I remember I got them cause you were pissed at me because I didn't call you when I got out of class.

MAX. Oh. Yeah.

B. Night.

MAX. Night.

B and MAX. Love you.

(MAX sits back down, smiling at her.)

E. You guys were together for two years, seriously?

B. On and off.

MAX. Mostly on…. See—the first time, I just—kissed her. We'd been friends for a really long time and I was so, SO stoned and looked at her and there was something different crawling around in her face. I wanted to kiss it. So I did.

We were in the parking lot of our old elementary school talking about soccer practice and chocolate milk and about that time we struck our hands down each other's pants in the back of the bus en route to the zoo.

At first when I kissed her—it was gonna be a thing we could laugh about later. Hey, remember that time we made out? That was fucking *funny.*

But then, it um, it began to accumulated from there. One day, I looked at her. She was cussing 'cause she'd just lit a little bit of her bangs on fire trying to light her cigarette. We were laying in the grass and the grass was all stuck in her hair and the way she cussed, it was like she always cussed, like she wasn't sure she was doing it right. And all of a sudden I looked at her and I loved her, 'cause it made sense to. And every time we made love—or whatever—it wasn't crazy or out of control or anything, but exactly how it was supposed to be. Not too soft and not too hard but fueled by everything she'd ever said. Every time she ever accidentally lit her hair on fire.

E. You guys were too married for your own good.

B. Sometimes. But at least if it were him we'd be here being mortified *together.*

E. I'm here.

(NURSE comes out.)

NURSE. Number six. Number six. Number six.

(NURSE leaves.)

B. Can this fucking be over with *please!*

E. Seriously.

B. They bring you in here and they....

E. They don't *bring* you in here, you come on your own accord.

B. And they ask you all these humiliating questions about your vagina and did you put this in your asshole, do you have sex with girls? And then it's all, pee in this cubic millimeter of a cup and then carry it through the waiting room with everyone watching you carry your own pee. Then they stick you with needles, and then you pass out 'cause all you can think about is how you might have AIDS or be pregnant. What if I'm really sick?

E. You're not.

B. But what if I am?

E. You're not.

B. What if *you* are?

E. I'm not.

B. How do you know?

E. I just know.

B. How?

E. You're annoying.

B. I'm *scared.*

E. This is just something you do. Like you get your teeth cleaned so they don't fall out. You get your twat checked so it doesn't fall out. It's not meant to freak you out so bad.

B. Thanks for doing it, too.

E. No problem.

B. You're not mad? About?

E. I'm not mad.

B. You're mad.

E. I'm not.

B. I didn't mean to call you a whore.

E. But you did.

B. No, I said, hey E, you should come.

E. You should come get tested with me because you're a gigantic whore.

B. I just didn't want to come alone. And, um.

E. What?

B. I love you, but.

E. But what?

B. You've had a lot of sex. With lots of different people.

E. What's a lot?

B. Plus all those guys in Europe.....

E. So? I like having sex.

B. How many—is it—now?

E. It doesn't matter.

B. When we graduated, it was three.

E. Four.

B. Oh, yeah, your cousin at the carnival.

E. He was my cousin's *friend*.

B. So how many now?

E. I don't know, I stopped counting, that's so Sex and the City.

B. You *are* Sex and the City. I mean, we are. All we ever talk about is who we've fucked or kissed and why the shoes they were wearing were stupid or good. I wanna talk about something else.

E. Like what?

B. I don't know. The current political climate.

E. Okay.

B. China is going to bomb the United States. New York and DC are gonna be gone in the next twenty years.

E. Neat.

B. Yeah. They're gonna drop nukes on us and we're all going to grow arms out of our foreheads.

(They sit in a depressed sad silence.)

E. Yeah, let's not talk about that.

(NURSE enters.)

NURSE. *(Boredly,)* Number nine. Number nine. Number NINE.

(No response. She leaves.)

B. *(Pause.)* So how many?

E. I don't *know*. I don't know.

(Two NURSES enter, fast, and stand adjacent to E and B, one with each of them. They carry clipboards, takes notes. The pace is quick.)

E. *(To her nurse)* Twenty-seven.

B. *(To her nurse)* Four.

E. *(To her nurse)* Just men.

B. *(To her nurse)* Is this confidential? Completely? *(Nurse nods.)* We just kissed a little. She was really pretty.

E. *(To her nurse)* Vaginal.

B. *(To her nurse, whispering)* Anal.

E. *(To her nurse)* Seven.

B. *(To her nurse)* Two. And a half.

E and B. *(To their nurses)* February 17th. Light. No.

B. *(To her nurse)* No. Never.

E. *(To her nurse)* Once. Miscarriage.

B and E. *(To their nurses)* Twenty-two.

E. *(to her nurse)* Jello.

B. *(To her nurse)* I try not to.

E. *(To her nurse)* ...My dog.

B. *(To her nurse)* Green.

E. *(To her nurse)* All the time.

B. *(To her nurse)* Never.

E. *(Pause. Shakes her head emphatically, seriously.)* Never.

(The NURSES leave. B and E sit in silence.)

E. I, um. I haven't really, actually. Been having it. Since I got back. Well not a lot.

B. But you did a lot, when you were there.

E. Not tons.

B. No, there was definitely at least that agent guy. That agent guy from LA.

E. Ew.

(KYLE stands up from behind them. Loud, annoying disco tech music and lights ensue.)

KYLE. *(Yelling over it)* ISN'T FLORENCE FUCKING SWEET?!

E. WHAT?!

KYLE. ISN'T FLORENCE FUCKING SWEET?!

E. YEAH! I'M SO DRUNK!

KYLE. I'M A CASTING AGENT IN LA!

E. COOL!

KYLE. WANNA SEE MY HOTEL ROOM?

E. OKAY!

(The music stops.)

B. And then?

E. And then to his hotel room, which as huge, where he did a lot of talking—I think.

KYLE. Hey. You kinda look like Kirstie Alley before she got fat.

E. … Thank you?

KYLE. I like you. You're not NICE. What girls need to understand is that nice is like your *mom.* I don't wanna fuck my mom. I don't wanna fuck a girl who wants to make me a sandwich and sing me a fairy tale and talk about my feelings—I want a bitch. Like a girl that'll take a piss in my shoes even if I'm good to her. No, wait. That's like—weird.

I mean a girl who'll key my car and fucking never call me back and I think I'm gonna die from wanting her so bad and not being able to figure her out. And just before I die—she calls. And just her voice over the pone—YEAH. That's the stuff. Just that push and pull—that—GRRR—fuck yeah. FUCK. YEAH. You are something else.

B. And then?

E. And then yadda yadda, and then in the morning, *(To KYLE, stretching)* Good morning.

KYLE. *(Groggy, sitting, slumping)* You gotta leave.

E. What?

KYLE. I said, you gotta go.

E. What's my name? *(KYLE laughs.)* What's my name? *(KYLE goes back to sleep.)* Yeah. I just really hope those pictures don't end up on the internet.

B. Ouch.

E. That'll turn you off.

B. So you haven't been?

E. Not really.

B. Ha. It's weird. We've switched places or something, you used to be the one having all the sex now I'm the one dragging you to the clinic.

E. I just, you know. Got sick of it. It gets pointless after while. You and whatever gentleman might as well be playing Nintendo but sweatier. It means nothing. I can't remember the last time it was any good.

B. You can't?

E. No. *(Remembering)* Paulo. .....Paulo.

(PAULO stands from behind them. He is sexy, Italian. Lights dim a bit as they speak to one another. They are somewhere else. E, remembering.)

E. Paulo,

welcome to the poem I am writing about you.

It will cover everything from your thick smell

to your kind eyes

to the fact that you like boats

and the fact that you wear a turtle around your neck

(a gift from the Last girl you Loved)

to the fact that I was wearing red to the croissants we stole in the morning

to the rocks that held us

to how your Big Italian Nose

became more and more endearing.

It will cover all these things,

and then some.

Welcome to the poem I am writing for you that you will never read.

PAULO. Ciao bella. Ciao *bella.Vourrei.* American.

E. Vourrei. Vourrei un biglietto.

PAULO. You need help? Eh?

E. Si. Yes. I, uh, biglietto del treno. I'm trying to get a ticket to Venice for Wednesday, Mercoledi, uh, on the treno. See the schedule says I need a reservation but I'm not sure and no one—no one will listen to me. No one'll help me.

PAULO. Paulo.

E. Elizabeth.

PAULO. *(Smiling, big and warm)* Bella.

(Lights shift back, but E continues to stare at PAULO.)

E. Right by the water. Cinque Terre. Northwestern Coast. The most beautiful. The most beautiful place I've ever seen. It wasn't just—it wasn't just that. We made love on the rocks like cave people. See they don't have sand there, not—

B. You've told me this.

E. Shut up, I'm painting a picture—it's not our idea of beaches, just rocks, big rocks, little rocks, everyone takes their clothes off and lays on them. Everyone from little kids to old people, everyone there is beautiful. They just sit outside all day by the water that's so clear it—it reflects your own thoughts back to you. Then you go inside at dusk and drink wine and talk about it.

You can hear everyone's forks and knives knocking really soft against somebody's grandmother's Venetian china if you sit outside and listen.

… He rented out sailboats for a living. He was real hairy with big blue eyes. Really nice jeans. We made love on the rocks. I'm not kidding. It was—it was the last time it meant, anything and I don't even know why.

PAULO. *(Quietly)* Ciao bella. *(Quieter)* Ciao.

B. Wow. No, it makes sense, you thought it was romantic so you didn't feel like a whore.

E. You need to quit calling me a whore.

B. I didn't the first time, you did.

E. Remind me why we're here, birthday girl?

B. Okay. Fine. Neither of us are whores.

(A nurse walks by. Shakes the TV. It begins to work again.. CONDOM MAN appears.)

CONDOM MAN. I am a condom, and I'm your friend. Don't be afraid of me. I come in numerous colors and flavors that make safe sex a juicy part of foreplay. Girls, you can learn to put me on with your *mouth*.

Fun! I am 89% effective for preventing pregnancy and the spread of STDS. See, watch my friends Jane and Sam, see what happens. All Jane needs to do is assert herself, just a little, and Sam will listen to her needs. I am your condom, and I am your friend.

(Cuts to SAM and JANE, HOT GUY and HOT GIRL, preferably inter-racial, making out.)

SAM. Oh, baby. Yeah. You taste real good.
JANE. Yeah. Sam, I like that, I like you on me, oh yeah.
SAM. Oh, smack, baby, yeah.
JANE. *(Stopping him.)* WAIT, Sam. Wait.
SAM. What, baby?
JANE. I think we should use—a CONDOM.
SAM. Oh baby, you're gonna play me like that?
JANE. Yes, Sam, I'm going to play you like that, because I play it *safe.*
SAM. Oh, come on, baby, we don't need all that.
JANE. No, Sam. We do need all that. And if you want some of this, we *have* to use protection.
SAM. ...Alright, baby.

(JANE smiles and winks at the camera. CUTS back to CONDOM MAN.)

CONDOM MAN. I am your condom, and I love you.

(TV freezes. B and E look at it, disgusted.)

E Yeah, condoms don't exist in fairytales. Or in Italy. Everyone smokes and no one dies.

(They sit in silence, again. E is somewhere else.)

B. Hey, E.
E. Hm?
B. Would you still be my friend if I had AIDS?

E. You don't have AIDS. People like us, we don't get AIDS, we just get—emotional complexes and eating disorders cause we feel used.

B. Oh.

(THE NURSE emerges)

NURSE. NUMBER 19. NUMBER 19. NUMBER 19.

B. *(As if bingo)* OOOH! OOOH! 19! That's me!

(She jumps up, waves her number in NURSE's face.) I'm number 19!!

NURSE. Results?

B. Yes.

NURSE. Follow me, please.

B. *(To E)* Wish me luck.

(B follows nurse, goes off. A few beats. E sits alone. From behind her, PAULO stands and approaches her.)

PAULO. Ciao, Elizabeth.

E. Ciao, Paulo.

(They move away from the clinic. We are on the beach, late at night. We hear the waves, see the moon, all of it: rocks, moonlit, an empty bottle of wine. They dance.)

PAULO. I think you are so beautiful.

E. *(Embarrassed)* Thank you. I like your pants.

PAULO. Pants?

E. Uh, your pants.

(She touches them.)

PAULO. Thank you. They are pants.

E. Yes, yes they are.

PAULO. You are a beautiful dance.

E. I bet you say that to all the drunk American girls.

PAULO. Yes?

E. No, you're supposed to say no.

PAULO. You like love, bella?

E. Oh, yes, I like love.

PAULO. You feel to me—scared. Do not be scared for me. I protect you.

E. I'm not scared.

PAULO. I want to take you on my boat, bella. It is a big red boat named after my sister, Anna. I want us to stay all day on the boat and I want us to swim together naked in the water and then I want us to sleep in the sun and look at all the old people in love and walking up the Via D'ell Amore and watch it move around the mountain. I want to make up stories of the old people and their love, yes? And then I want to make for you dinner. And then I want to hold you.

E. I'm—I'm supposed to leave tomorrow.

PAULO. Then I think—then I think we will have to make love tonight.

E. Right here? But—

PAULO. *(Stopping her)* Shhhh. Bella.

(He kisses her. They sink to the ground.
B re-enters. Lights resume, we're back in the clinic. PAULO is gone.
   B gives a big stupid thumbs up, all smiles. Goes to E, who is still
   somewhere else.)

E. I miss love. I wanna be in love.

(The NURSE enters.)

NURSE. Number twenty. Number twenty. Number 20.

B. E, that's you, number 20.

E. Yeah.

B. I'll be here.

E. Okay.

(E follows the nurse.
B takes a seat back in her chair, so relieved, swinging her feet. Watches the
TV. A GAY MAN, obviously in his thirties, speaks.)

GAY MAN. Hi, my name is Charlie and I am an eighteen-year-old boy and I am gay. I just got my results—I do not have AIDS or HIV or any sexually transmitted disease at all. PHEW. That was CLOSE! Chances are, you don't either. Give yourself a pat on the back. Go ahead, do it! *(Pause.)*
But, I've had friends that have gotten sick. Some of them are just seventeen years old, which is younger than me. I am eighteen. I've learned to support them, and though at first it's scary to hang out with them at the skating rink or the arcade, it only reminds me that I need to be careful when I select my partners. What if my partner were to get sick one day? I have to be informed. Feel free to take a pamphlet on your way out to keep informed, and stay cool. Stay cool. Stay cool. Stay Cool. Stay Cool.

(A NURSE walks by and smacks the TV; it goes to static. From the static, E re-enters, slowly, stunned. Staring ahead.)

B. What? What's wrong?

(E moves to PAULO, stops, and looks at him.)

PAULO. Mi Scusi. Mi scusi. Mi scusi.

(E keeps looking at him as the TV drones with static, this sound overwhelming the space as lights go to black. Lights.)

End of play

PISCHER

by

Ted Nusbaum

CHARACTERS

ELON: mid twenties, a yeshiva student. Naive, sincere, easily manipulated.

SASHA: late twenties to early thirties, a Russian immigrant. Cynic and secular Jew. Explosives expert.

AVRAM: late twenties to early thirties, a zealot. Charismatic, calm, calculated. The brains behind the operation.

SETTING

The play takes place in the secret backroom of an air conditioning company in East Jerusalem, Israel.

TIME

The present day.

(A workshop light casts an ominous shadow over the room. Air conditioners and their parts lay about in disarray. At center, SASHA, 30's, sits at a table working on the hull of a large air conditioner. Three quick knocks sound at the door. He stops, moves cautiously to the entrance and speaks.)

SASHA. Mee zeh?
ELON. It's Elon!

(SASHA opens the door, drags ELON, 20's, into the room.)

SASHA. What the fuck are you doing?
ELON. What do you mean? I was told to come at 4 in the morning—it's 4 in the morn—
SASHA. I ask, 'who is it?' What do you do?

(SASHA knocks three times against the door.)

ELON. Sorry.
SASHA. What the fuck is sorry? You haven't been here two minutes and already you've screwed up.
ELON. Sorry, Sasha. My head's not straight ... you know.

(SASHA sits at the table.)

SASHA. You better get your head straight or you can turn around and go home.
ELON. I'm not going anywhere until we get the guy who got David. That's the deal.
SASHA. Maybe you're not up to it, Pischer.

69

ELON Avram thinks I am.

SASHA. Avram isn't perfect.

ELON. You don't worship him anymore?

SASHA. *(Points)* Hand me those pliers? *(ELON reaches for the pliers but accidentally knocks the flashlight over.)* You have the hands of a Yeshiva student—good for only two things: praying and jerking off.

ELON. I don't jerk off!

SASHA. I've seen the Vaseline you boys keep around—I'm sure it's not a case of chapped lips.

ELON. The Torah says—

SASHA. *(Curses in Russian) Bla bla bla*, the Torah.

ELON. You don't observe, Sasha?

SASHA. I observe, Elon, but from very far away.

ELON. Avram knows this? Where is he anyway?

SASHA. Listen, what Avram knows about me is between me and Avram. *(Re: the mess in the room)* Now do something productive and clean up this mess. I'm already regretting we allowed you to come. *(Snaps pliers)* Don't stick your Jew nose where it doesn't belong or I'll twist it off!

ELON. We? I know who makes the decisions around here.

(ELON deposits objects around the room into a bucket making a racket.)

SASHA. Stop making so much noise.

ELON. *(Stops his work)* Come on Sasha, give me something real to do.

SASHA. Keep your voice down.

ELON. I didn't come here to clean up junk!

SASHA. Shhh! You want Shin Bet to hear you? *(ELON works more quietly now.)* You can't be so emotional.

ELON. He was killed two days ago!

SASHA. I know it's been tough. He was a good friend.

ELON. He may have been your friend, but don't forget, Sasha, he was my brother.

SASHA. Elon, don't lecture me on the subject of loss. Have you forgot who you're talking to?

ELON. I just can't believe he's gone, Sasha. *(Beat)* I keep thinking about our first summer here. I was thirteen, David was sixteen, and we saw the entire country in the back of an Egged bus. Masada, Eliat, Jerusalem ... it was the best summer of my life and I spent it with him.

SASHA. I'm sorry, Elon.

ELON. It's pretty ironic that he got killed on a bus, huh.

SASHA. I don't know—I'm not a philosopher.

ELON. It's not philos—

SASHA. Shhh! *(SASHA hears something outside. He moves to the door and listens carefully.)* You left okay? No one saw you?

ELON. I don't think so.

SASHA. What's that supposed to mean?

ELON. I don't have eyes in the back of my head.

SASHA. You damn well better grow eyes in the back of your head!

ELON. No one saw me.

SASHA. If you fuck this up because of your typical *schumckiness*—

ELON. I've changed.

SASHA. People don't change that much.

ELON. I'll pull the trigger myself—you watch.

SASHA. I doubt that.

ELON. You don't think I can do it?

SASHA. No, Pischer, I don't. But in the morning, we'll see what you're made of. *(Suddenly, there are three quick knocks at the door. SASHA dims the lights and moves to the keyhole.)* Mee zeh?

(There are three more knocks—slow and deliberate—and SASHA opens the door to reveal AVRAM, 30's, charismatic, calm, intense. He enters with two black gym bags and shuts the door behind him.)

AVRAM. How are we doing?

SASHA. We are getting there.

AVRAM. *(Unhappy with the progress)* The van is in the alley— we have 30 *minutes.*

ELON. Avram, what's his name?

AVRAM. Later, Pischer. *(To SASHA)* It looks heavy.

SASHA. It's not so bad.

ELON. *(To AVRAM)* I'm going to spit in his face before we kill him.

(AVRAM silences him with his index finger.)

AVRAM. *(To SASHA)* Lift it. *(ELON goes to lift it—SASHA stops him, tries to himself but can't. He motions ELON to help and together, they barely lift it.)* Not a three man job, Sasha? *(They gladly put it down.)* When did you get so fat, anyway?

SASHA. I am not fat.

(AVRAM pulls out various objects from the gym bag: three jumpsuits, a rolled up towel, a map, and an exacto knife.)

AVRAM. It's all my wife's challah you eat on the Sabbath. You're like the calf before Mt. Horeb—

ELON. Avram, please. Who killed David?

AVRAM. Can I see your driver's license, Pischer?

(ELON opens his wallet and produces his license. AVRAM snatches it away, goes to the table and slices into it with the exacto knife.)

ELON. What are you doing?!

AVRAM. Trust in Hashem, it will all work out.

ELON. I do trust Hashem. He has brought me here for a purpose.

SASHA. Would you shut up already?

AVRAM. Sasha, please.

SASHA. His voice is giving me a headache.

ELON. Is it my voice, Sasha, or every time I bring up Hashem you suddenly get a headache?

SASHA. I am warning you, Elon.

ELON. *(Under his breath)* Hellenist.

SASHA. Excuse me?

ELON. He is barely even a Jew, Avram!

SASHA. Who the fuck does he think he is?

AVRAM. He is the Pischer.

SASHA. I don't care if he's David Ben Gurion!

ELON. Now that was a good Jew!

AVRAM. Quiet! Do you want Shin Bet to hear you? *(To ELON)* There is something you must understand. The path of Hashem is an ingenious one. Who says He isn't working through the Hellenist and the Tzadik alike to bring about the coming of the Messiah?

ELON. I haven't thought about it that way, Avram.

SASHA. Maybe if you spent less time in the bathroom with the Vaseline—

AVRAM. Tut! Enough. Everything happens through Hashem, whether one knows it or not. *(Turning on SASHA)* Surely you must grant that much, Sasha.

SASHA. *(Sarcastic)* So we get slaughtered in cafes and discos because God wants it that way?

AVRAM. Who says it's not part of the bigger picture?

SASHA. I don't know, Avram—I'm not a philosopher.

AVRAM. Trust me, Sasha, Hashem is working through you whether you like it or not.

SASHA. He must know as much about initiators and switches as I do then!

ELON. It's a bomb?

(AVRAM flashes a look at SASHA.)

AVRAM. Yes, Pischer. Sasha is making a bomb.

ELON. Who's the target?

AVRAM. Can you drive a van?

ELON. I can drive anything you want.

AVRAM. Fine, but have you driven a van before?

ELON. Not really.

SASHA. *(In Russian)* Oh, brother.

ELON. I'm sure it's not so difficult.

SASHA. No, not at all. The two of us in back, a half-ton of explosives ... if you hit a single pothole or run us up against a curb, say good night. *(To AVRAM)* This is a bad idea.

ELON. I'm sure I can do it.

SASHA. He's sure—I feel so much better now.

AVRAM. Sasha! I could swear you have a job to do. *(AVRAM leads ELON to a black gym bag and zips it open.)* Pischer, put those boxes into the air conditioner.

(ELON begins placing the boxes into the hull of the air conditioner but something stops him.)

ELON. We're using nails?

AVRAM. What?

ELON. What are we doing with nails and screws?

AVRAM. You know the big shots don't travel by themselves. We go after his car, we have to get everyone inside, just to make sure.

ELON. Whose car? You still haven't told me who we're going after.

AVRAM. Patience, Pischer.

ELON. I think I have a right to know.

AVRAM. Is there really a difference between one Arab and another? They all want the same thing—your extinction.

ELON. I'm sure they don't all want that.

AVRAM. Are you in love, Pischer?

ELON. What?

AVRAM. Do you love them?

ELON. Who?

AVRAM. Do you love the Arabs?

ELON. Very funny.

AVRAM. Do you have an Arab girlfriend?

ELON. What?

AVRAM. Do you have sex with Arab girls?

ELON. Avram!

AVRAM. How do you know who you're screwing when they wear those ridiculous veils?

ELON. That's disgusting—

AVRAM. Why do you want to protect them, Pischer? Hamas—they want to push us into the sea! They don't even recognize our right to exist! You know what that means? Five thousand years of Jewish history is suddenly negotiable? Is a myth? Like they say the Holocaust is?! *(Beat)* You know where I was yesterday? While you were safely tucked away in your library, I was building the new road which will link Kiryat Arbah to Tekoah. Something happened yesterday, Pischer. We were digging into an old hillside and we came across a tract of very old looking stones. We carefully began to remove them, one by one, and you know what we found? An enormous pit! They lowered me down and there was a mikva—and a key! And the key matched up to others found during the time of the Second Temple! Don't you see, everywhere we turn, as far as the eye can see, Jews have been living on this land for thousands of years! They want to say Israel doesn't exist? I say, look at historical fact! They say Jerusalem is their capital? I say again, look at historical fact! The resistance to occupation—their occupation of our land— starts tonight, in this little basement, with the three of us and concludes in a few hours when our target is in flames.

(AVRAM looks overcome.)

ELON. Avram?

SASHA. He's fine, Elon. Give him a moment.

AVRAM. It's not that what I'm saying is an easy thing. Taking a human life is a grave matter. *(Suppresses a smile)* It changes you. Wouldn't you agree, Sasha?

SASHA. Like I said, I'm not a philosopher.

AVRAM. He doesn't want to admit it, but it changes you—for the better. Why remain an insignificant Pischer when you can be so much more? *(Off ELON's reaction)* Don't look at me like I'm telling you something you don't know. We're all insignificant until we *do* something.

ELON. All I'm saying is I don't love the idea of spraying nails and screws around. It's sloppy. And random. And cruel. It's what they do. You said we're going after one man, now suddenly, you tell me it may be a few more? I don't know what to believe.

SASHA. Stop being such a Jew, Elon.

ELON. What's that supposed to mean?

SASHA. It means stop being weak.

ELON. I am not weak, Sasha.

(SASHA and AVRAM exchange a knowing look.)

SASHA. *(To AVRAM)* Maybe he's Shin Bet.

AVRAM. Pischer?

SASHA. He loves the Arabs.

AVRAM. Is this true?

ELON. I don't love the Arabs.

SASHA. I think he's Shin Bet.

AVRAM. Maybe he's here to set us up.
SASHA. If he's Shin Bet, he's as good as dead.
ELON. I am not Shin Bet.

(SASHA grabs a cordless power drill, and alongside AVRAM, slowly corners ELON downstage.)

AVRAM. Tell us, Pischer, why would you go and join Shin Bet like that?
ELON. I am not Shin Bet!
SASHA. He is too dumb to be Shin Bet.
AVRAM. Or is he too smart?
ELON. How many times do I have to tell you, I'm not Shin Bet!
SASHA. We didn't do anything to you.
AVRAM. We love you, Pischer.
SASHA. You're our new best friend.
AVRAM. Part of the crew.
SASHA. One of the boys.
AVRAM. On the team.
SASHA. On our side.
AVRAM. Not theirs.
ELON. Are you serious?
SASHA. His left eye flutters—he is lying.
ELON. I have a nervous twitch!
AVRAM. Come now, before you regret it, who contacted you?
ELON. I would never do that.
AVRAM. Why are you making this difficult? Tell us, before it's too late—who are you working for?
ELON. I'm not working for anyone!
SASHA. He's lying!
ELON. I am not!
AVRAM. We know the truth.
ELON. What truth?
AVRAM. Who you're working for!
ELON. Avram, please—

(SASHA drives ELON's head into the bucket, lowering the drill to his

temple.)

AVRAM. *Okay* Sasha—
SASHA. Who are you working for?
AVRAM. That's enough—
SASHA. Who are you working for!
ELON. Lemme go—
SASHA. *(In Russian)* WHO ARE YOU WORKING FOR?!
ELON. I want to go home!!!

(ELON breaks into impassioned prayer. AVRAM finally pulls SASHA away.)

AVRAM. That's enough, Sasha. He's ready.
SASHA. We should let him go, Avram. He's had enough.

(ELON stumbles sway from the bucket, collecting himself.)

ELON. *(Recovering)* I'm not sure I want to do this anymore.
AVRAM. Is that right, Pischer, you're going to walk out of here without honoring David?
SASHA. We can do the job ourselves.
AVRAM. *(To ELON)* Maybe you're not here for David after all?
ELON. Why else would I be here?
AVRAM. Oh, I don't know. Maybe you're looking for someone to replace him.
ELON. What?
AVRAM. Is it going to be me—or Sasha? If you ask me, I look a lot more like David than Sasha does.
ELON. You're not funny.
AVRAM. Don't you want to avenge his murder, Pischer? *(Beat)* Doesn't it say in Nachum that the Lord is a zealous and avenging God? Didn't King David say in Psalms that the righteous man will rejoice when he sees the vengeance? *(Beat)* Don't you want to be a righteous man, Pischer? *(Beat)* David is gone and he's not coming back. So is my daughter. So is Sasha's wife. We honor their memories by taking action and it's only through action that we will deter future

attacks

SASHA. With all due respect, Avram, this will not deter future attacks.

AVRAM. It will make them think twice.

SASHA. *(Sarcastic)* About how many bombers to send out—two or three?

AVRAM. It sends a very clear message. You attack us, we will return the favor.

SASHA. That is fine, Avram, but do you really think it will stop them?

AVRAM. If I didn't know you any better, I'd say you're scared, Sasha.

SASHA. *(Laughs)* Me? That's a good one.

AVRAM. Why can't you see that what we are doing will be remembered for generations to come?

SASHA. I can't see that far into the future, okay?

(ELON suddenly breaks the tension by dumping a box of nails into the air conditioner.)

ELON. Are we going to talk all night or are we going to do this?

(AVRAM swells with pride. He squeezes ELON's shoulder warmly. All three return to their work with a fevered and concentrated pitch. ELON with the nails and screws, SASHA with the air conditioner, and AVRAM who flashes ELON's license and bestows it in a ceremonial manner.)

AVRAM. You are now Yitzak Rosenbaum. You live at 12 Natan Straus in Mea Shearim. You have a wife named Chani and two daughters, Eliza and Shira. *(AVRAM stuffs the van keys into Elon's pocket.)* If we get pulled over simply say you are delivering air conditioners to the settlement at Tekoah. You will remain calm but with a hint of agitation in your eye as if their stopping you will make you late and if you are late you'll be fired and if you're fired, who will feed your wife and children?

(ELON nods.)

AVRAM. Sasha, what's left?

SASHA. Just a quick run through and then we can load the van. Come on, don't be shy. *(They approach and he points into the air conditioner.)* This is the initiator. This is the anti-open switch. And this is the fusing system. I'm fucking good, no?

ELON. *(Points)* Is that the timer?

SASHA. *(Slaps his hand)* Don't touch. Yes, that's the timer. *(Looks at AVRAM)* 7:35?

AVRAM. Exactly. Our man is punctual.

SASHA. Now just in case we're delayed, see these wires—one, two, and three? The only way to defuse the package is to clip all the wires simultaneously. Don't fuck this part up because if you clip any single wire by itself, it's going to get real ugly in about 60 seconds. Got it?

(They both nod.)

AVRAM. Let's look at the map. *(AVRAM spreads open the map as ELON looks on.)* We're going to wind up Jericho road, go right on El-Mansuriya, and come in the back way onto Raba El-Adawiya. This way, we bypass the checkpoint at the Dome of Ascension.

ELON. I know this road! You can see all the way to the Dead Sea from this middle school—

AVRAM. So you know it?

ELON. Know what?

AVRAM. The target.

(AVRAM folds up the map and sticks it in Elon's pocket.)

ELON. The school is the target?

AVRAM. The drop off circle.

SASHA. Your man, Elon, the sweet, sensitive family man who blew your brother's bus to bits? He'll be dropping off his kids at 7:35 in the morning.

ELON. His children?

(ELON reacts silently for a moment.)

AVRAM. Look, I wish he would come out of hiding and say, hello everybody, here I am! Come and get me! But guess what, he doesn't. We just happen to know he'll be here at this time, in a couple of hours, and here is our chance. Are you going to be the one to fuck it up?

ELON. We're going to kill his kids?

AVRAM, We're not deliberately targeting them.

ELON. It seems pretty deliberate to me.

SASHA. There were children on your brother's bus, Elon. What's fair is fair.

ELON. There were?

AVRAM. Yes, Pischer. Four died and three more were injured. One lost her legs.

(ELON looks sick to his stomach.)

SASHA. If one, maybe two get caught in the explosion, it's unfortunate, but also necessary.

ELON. The Talmud says that every life is an entire universe. Every life matters.

AVRAM. And the Torah doesn't discriminate between civilians and the military in a time of war. Which source takes precedence— man's or God's? *(Beat)* You must see the bigger picture. One day, these children you want to save will strap explosives to themselves and walk into a cafe where you're having a nice lunch with your future wife and children. Can't you see how we are saving Jewish lives at this very moment?

ELON. But that's all we have—the present moment. You can't act according to some future that may never come to be.

AVRAM. For Godsakes, Elon, be a man! For once in your insignificant life, be the thing that David hoped you'd become—a real flesh and blood man!

ELON. I am a man.

AVRAM. No, you're a boy who wants to be a man but wanting isn't enough. *(Beat)* I was there, Pischer, did you know that? Long after the cameras and the reporters left, I was there, cleaning up. I volunteer—it keeps things fresh—and if you saw what I saw—what was left of him—

ELON. *(Overlapping)* Please! Stop!

AVRAM. *(Removes something from pocket)* I found this 15 meters from the bus. Still attached to his finger. *(ELON covers his ears but AVRAM rakes ELON's hands away.)* Listen to me, Pischer. I knew it was his arm because the sleeve matched up to the shirt he was wearing and I recognized the scar on his right hand—the one he got leaping over that fence in Ramat Gan.

(AVRAM hands the object to ELON.)

ELON. His ring.

AVRAM. I was going to give it you later, but you should have it now.

SASHA. We have five minutes.

(ELON takes the ring and cups it in his hands. He is moved by having this small piece of his brother back in his possession.

AVRAM motions to SASHA who unwraps the bundled up towel that has been sitting on the table since Avram's arrival. Inside it is a bottle of vodka. The stage is completely clear except for the hull of the air conditioner which lies down center. SASHA has placed the towel atop it as a kind of altar.

SASHA pulls out a photograph and looks at it, cradling it to his chest, he recites something in Russian and downs the shot of vodka. SASHA fills the glass and offers it to AVRAM who pulls out a little girl's necklace. He caresses the chain a moment, recites a prayer in Hebrew then takes the shot of vodka. He fills the glass and hands it to ELON.)

AVRAM. *(Checks his watch)* Go ahead, Pischer, it's time to say something. *(ELON waits a moment before speaking, fiddling with David's ring. He steps away from the air conditioner.)* Pischer—

ELON. This is not a Jewish act.

AVRAM. Will you disregard the commands of the Torah?

ELON. David would never do a thing like this.
AVRAM. David was a real man!
ELON. I'm sorry, Avram, but I can't.
AVRAM. Pischer, you don't want to do this.
ELON. Yes, Avram, I do.

(AVRAM removes a pistol from beneath his shirt.)

ELON. What are you doing to do? Kill me?
AVRAM. You know too much.
ELON. What about all that business about taking human lives and how hard it is? You're going to kill me? You're a hypocrite, Avram, and a liar.
AVRAM. And you are nothing but a cowardly Jew. I am ashamed of you. *(Beat)* Sasha, take care of him.

(AVRAM hands the pistol to SASHA.)

SASHA. It's just Pischer, Avram.
AVRAM. You heard me. Deal with this Pischer.
SASHA. He won't talk. Right, Elon, you won't say anything?

(ELON is silent.)

AVRAM. For the last time, are you with us, Pischer, or not? *(ELON removes a small prayer book from his pocket and begins praying.)* Now will you do your job or will I have do it for you?
SASHA. I want no part of this.
AVRAM. You disappoint me, Sasha. *(AVRAM wrenches the pistol from SASHA's hands. ELON reacts. Looks down at the air conditioner, sticks his hand into the open latch, and yanks a wire out for all to see. AVRAM and SASHA freeze.)* What's happening?
SASHA. Jesus Christ, Elon. *(To AVRAM)* We have to get out of here.
AVRAM. What?
SASHA. We have to get out of here!

(SASHA backpedals for the door as AVRAM trains the pistol on ELON, closes in on him, then suddenly backhands ELON with the pistol, sending him to the ground.

AVRAM fishes the van keys out of his pocket and starts away. Stops. Returns and spits in ELON's face before following SASHA out the door. The sound of the door being bolted is heard. ELON comes to—sprints to the door and tries it but it won't open. He bangs on it several times.)

ELON. Avram! Somebody! Help!

(The sound of the van engine turns over and then the van peals away, fading into the distance. He bangs on the door harder now. Several panicked blows. Then suddenly, he stops. Turns to the air conditioner as the sound of ticking rises in the background.)

(Blackout.)

End of Play

COSTUME PLOT

ELON: A white, button-down dress shirt, black pants, black shoes, tzi-tzi, a black kipa (yarmulke) (black suit jacket is optional).

SASHA: worn jeans (no holes), soccer-style zippered warm up jacket, dark sneakers.

AVRAM: flannel shirt, jeans, colored, knit kipa (yarmulke), tzi-tzit, hiking boots.

PROPERTY PLOT

Partly constructed pipe bomb
Several spools of different colored wire (yellow, red, blue, green)
Several roles of duct tape, electrical tape, masking tape
Bucket
Folding table
Folding chair
Various and random pieces of metal tubing, fittings, housings
Several boxes of nails
Several boxes of screws
Timer
Flashlight
Large work light with extension cord
Emptied and extra-large air conditioner hull (for placement of bomb)

HAND PROPS

Bottle of vodka
Shot glass
Cloth or towel (which concealed the vodka)
Small copy of Torah – to fit in one's back pocket (Elon's)
Van keys
Driver's license (Elon's)
Exacto knife
Map
Cordless drill
Pliers and various tools
Army issue hand gun
      Three black gym bags

RELATIONTRIP

by

Sharyn Rothstein

RelationTrip was first produced by The Vital Theatre Company in March, 2006. The play was directed by Catherine Ward. The cast was as follows:

CARRIE	Zakiyyah Alexander
JULIE	Nedra McClyde
ERIC	William Jackson Harper
OWEN	Jason Updike

ABOUT THE AUTHOR

Sharyn Rothstein is a member of Youngblood, ensemble Studio Theatre's collective for emerging playwrights under the age of thirty. Three of her short plays will be published in the 2005 and 2006 editions of Smith & Kraus' *The Best Ten Minute Plays for 3 or More Actors*. Sharyn's full-length and one-act plays have been workshopped and/or produced at the Ensemble Studio Theatre, the Vital Theatre, Soho Think Tank, Manhattan Theatre Source, Makor/92nd Street Y, as part of the New York International Fringe Festival, and at numerous theatres around New York by talented young production companies.

CHARACTERS

ERIC; twenties, Carrie's boyfriend
CARRIE: twenties, Eric's girlfriend
JULIE: Carrie's sister
OWEN: twenties

SETTING

A train going to Carrie and Julie's cousin's wedding.

(A train. ERIC and CARRIE, boyfriend-girlfriend, and Carrie's sister, JULIE, with sunglasses and a headache, enter the train with their bags and move themselves into seats while they speak.)

ERIC. I don't think I've been on a train in forever.

JULIE. My god, why is it so bright in here? It's painful.

ERIC. I believe they call it sunlight, Jules.

JULIE. Well can't they turn it off? Some of us have a hangover.

CARRIE. I think it's gorgeous.

JULIE. I'm putting my bag on the seat so nobody sits here.

ERIC. *(To CARRIE, overlapping JULIE)* When was the last time we were on a train?

JULIE. *(Overlapping)* I know I'm gonna get, you guys are gonna *cuddle* the whole trip and I'm gonna get some painful looking dude with chronic bad breath ...

CARRIE. *(To ERIC, overlapping JULIE)* I don't know if we ... I can't even remember ever *being* on a train with you.

JULIE. *(Continued)* ... and a history of molesting small children and *animals* or something. *(ERIC and CARRIE exchange a good-humored glance over Julie's tirade. We hear the train leave the station in the background.)* This is pretty typical Jeremy. Get married someplace so far upstate it's practically in another country even though *you* live in the city with everybody else you know. *(Beat)* Jesus, I can't believe he's getting married.

(From behind their seats, OWEN, attractive, in his mid-to-late twenties, leans over the back of his seat.)

OWEN. I'm sorry to interrupt but you said Jeremy, right? Jeremy Ellis?

JULIE. Yeah, that's who—He's our cousin. Well, *(indicating her and CARRIE) our* cousin—

OWEN. That's crazy. I'm going there too. We were college buddies. When I got the invite, all of our friends from college we're like:
of *course* he's making us go to the middle of nowhere. He's such a
weirdo.

JULIE. *(Simultaneous with OWEN)* He's such a weirdo—

OWEN. *(Laughing)* I'm Owen.

JULIE. Julie.

CARRIE. Carrie, her sister.

ERIC. Eric. Nice to meet you man.

OWEN. Hey, you mind if I...?

*(Owen indicates moving next to JULIE. JULIE moves her bag off the
seat—quickly.)*

JULIE. No, not at all. Not at *all*. Take a seat. Sit down. Please.
Please, sit down.

OWEN. I can't believe he's biting the bullet, you know? I never
thought he'd go so early. In school, man, he was *crazy*. He had a different girlfriend for every semester *and* one from every dorm. *(JULIE
laughs)* But I guess it's a while since college, right?

ERIC. Yup.

JULIE. And he has known her forever.

OWEN. Right? But the weird thing is, he never talked about her
before they started dating. I'd never even heard of her, and then it
turns out she's like one of his best friends or something.

ERIC. So he was probably embarrassed about her.

CARRIE. Eric!

ERIC. What? C'mon, why wouldn't a guy like Jeremy talk about
a girl like Susan to his buddies at college?

CARRIE. Yeah but you don't need to *say* it.

ERIC. "Sorry". I just hope they've got some actual chemistry and
it's not all just they were good friends and he got lonely or something.

CARRIE. Jesus Eric.

ERIC. What?

CARRIE. Nothing. Just promise you won't make any toasts,
okay?

ERIC. *(Playfully)* Why? Are you afraid I'm gonna embarrass you

Carrie?

CARRIE. *(Also playful)* I *know* you're going to embarrass me. You're an embarrassing *person.*

ERIC. *(Still playfully)* Oh really? Then you must find it *very* embarrassing that you're so unbelievably in *love* with me, huh?

(ERIC tickles her. She squirms, laughing.)

CARRIE. Get away from me. You're such a *child.* Eric—
ERIC. If you want me to stop you've gotta kiss me.
CARRIE. No.
ERIC. Yes.
CARRIE. Eric, we're on a train. There are people here.
ERIC. I don't care. Kiss me.
CARRIE. No.
ERIC. Kiss me or else.

(ERIC tickles her harder.)

CARRIE. *(Struggling and laughing)* Fine! Fine I'll kiss you you *jerk*!

(They kiss. For a while. They stop. They gaze into each other's eyes. OWEN and JULIE look at each other: gross.)

JULIE. *So...*
OWEN. I take it you two are together...?
ERIC. Sorry. Carrie couldn't help it.

(CARRIE swats at him.)

CARRIE. Shut up!
JULIE. Both of you shut up, please. Or at least... keep your mouths *closed.*
CARRIE. *Sorry.* And anyway, *Eric,* just because they've been

friends forever doesn't mean they don't have chemistry together.

ERIC. I'm not saying that's what it means, I'm just saying I hope they *do* have chemistry cause it's never gonna last if they don't.

OWEN. I don't know, it sounds like he really likes her…

ERIC. That's good.

CARRIE. Why wouldn't it last? Plenty of marriages that don't have chemistry, or I guess a better word is … what would a better word be for it?

ERIC. *(Grabbing her dramatically)* Passion.

CARRIE. *(Laughing)* Yeah, passion. Plenty of marriages that don't have passion work.

OWEN. That's true. In some countries passion—or even love—doesn't even enter in the equation. I read this book, *The Exile of Love—*

JULIE. Hey, I read that book!

OWEN. *(Excited)* Yeah?

CARRIE. I think I read that too—

OWEN. *(To JULIE)* Hey, what'd you think of the part—

JULIE. With the Eskimos?

OWEN. Yeah! That was—

CARRIE. Banal and repetitive?

JULIE. *(Over CARRIE)* Totally unbelievable—!

OWEN. Right?

ERIC. Okay but we're not talking about Eskimos. We're talking about Americans, and in America Love Reigns Supreme. That's what everybody's looking for, right? Hot, crazy, passionate love. And I just think if you don't get it you're always gonna wonder and then things go bad.

CARRIE. Well maybe, but friendship, I think that a love based on friendship and deep trust is a lot tougher and can last a lot longer than just a passionate love.

ERIC. I don't think so, Carrie. My parents have been married over thirty years and it's because, I really think it's *because* they're still passionate about each other. Even when they fight, you can tell, they're crazy about each other.

OWEN. My parents never fight.

CARRIE. Your parents never fight?

JULIE. Never?

OWEN. No. Well, yeah. Once. They fought once.

ERIC. What'd they fight about?

OWEN. Whether to neuter the cat.

JULIE. Who won?

ERIC. Who *lost*?

OWEN. The cat.

JULIE. Our parents fought a lot.

CARRIE. They didn't fight *a lot*, Julie.

JULIE. No, you're right. They fought *constantly*.

(ERIC laughs.)

CARRIE. That's not true. Maybe you don't remember, but there were times when they were good together. I think when our parents' marriage worked—*when* it worked—it was because they were committed to each other. They loved each other in this deeply loyal way.

JULIE. Our parent's marriage *didn't* work, Carrie.

CARRIE. That's because they *stopped* being loyal to each other.

OWEN. Well I mean they don't have to be mutually exclusive do they? You *can* have loyalty and passion.

JULIE. Of course you can—

OWEN. I mean it's not impossible—

CARRIE. No one's saying it's *impossible*, it's just not very realistic.

ERIC. Well of course it's not realistic if you don't *think* it's realistic.

CARRIE. Oh please. This isn't about some self-fulfilling whatever, it's about *reality*. It's about how in *reality* people get fat, they get wrinkly and *spotted*—maybe not *your* parents, granted—but a *lot* of people—and if you're not getting married cause you're going to commit—I mean a really kind of *transcendent* commitment—to someone on this very *loyal*, this other-person-first way... I'm just saying, if it's based on *passion*, if it's based on just *sex*, it's never gonna work.

ERIC. Sex isn't important to you?

JULIE. It's important to me.

OWEN. *(To JULIE)* Me too,

CARRIE. Of course it's *important* to me ... now. I'm *young*. But when I get older, when I have *kids* to take care of—

ERIC. Oh man that is such a cliché.

CARRIE. It's a cliché because it's *true*. I mean, what about if it isn't the kids, or the job or whatever, what if it's illness? Or loss? Or something you hope will *never* happen to you—like you get bladder control issues—

JULIE. That *will* never happen to me—

CARRIE. Or you get depression, or cancer or just even anger?

OWEN. Well, I don't think—

ERIC. I never realized what a pessimist you are.

CARRIE. These things *happen*. And lesser things. Like what if you just aren't attracted to each other anymore? What if you just can't get excited for this person anymore?

ERIC. Then you *leave*.

OWEN. Well I don't think—

JULIE. It's not that simple—

CARRIE. You leave? You just leave, that's it? No sex, no attraction—so: goodbye.

ERIC. Yes.

CARRIE. You've got a *house* together, you've got—I mean, what if you've got *kids*?

ERIC. Your kids aren't going to be happy if you're not.

CARRIE. Oh that's great.

JULIE. Eric, you really think that?

CARRIE. That's the most self-centered, fucked-up thing I've ever heard you say.

ERIC. *Why?* It's *true*. When your—can you honestly tell me that when your parents were fighting and your dad was coming home late-a little too late every night—

JULIE. Eric—

OWEN. Hey, man—

ERIC. —you really think you were happy? I mean, were you really *happy* then?

CARRIE. I can't believe you just said that.

ERIC. I'm asking you a question, Carrie. When your parents

were making each other miserable—were you happy? Julie? Were you happy?

JULIE. Eric that's really not, I don't want to talk about that right now.

ERIC. Why? That's what we're discussing isn't it? Can your kids be happy if you're completely miserable?

CARRIE. In front of my *sister*. And someone we don't even *know*.

ERIC. It's a *discussion*. It's not like I brought it up out of nowhere, it's not like it doesn't *fit*. You're the one talking about loyalty, about staying together for the kids. So I'm asking you—I don't know, my parents never got divorced, so I'm asking *you*: What's it like when your parents aren't having sex? Or aren't even attracted to each other? What's it like when your parents don't love each other anymore?

(Beat)

OWEN. Hey, Eric, let's just…

ERIC. What?

OWEN. Calm down a little okay?

CARRIE. You know *nothing* about my parents.

ERIC. Really?

CARRIE. Really.

ERIC. Because I've been with you for over two years. I think I *know* your parents, Carrie. I mean, I've never seen them in the same *room* together, but that's because they can't stand each other.

CARRIE. My parents love each other very much.

JULIE. Carrie—

CARRIE. Julie, stay out of this.

JULIE. Why? They're my parents too.

CARRIE. This isn't about you. Not everything is about you.

JULIE. Wow.

CARRIE. I just meant—

JULIE. Mom and dad do *not* love each other very much and you know it. In fact, I don't think they ever really did.

CARRIE. You don't know what you're talking about.

JULIE. I know *exactly* what I'm talking about.

ERIC. It's not a *secret*, Carrie. They've been divorced since you were in middle school.

CARRIE. That doesn't mean they don't love each other. That they *didn't* love each other.

ERIC. So they loved each other.

JULIE. No.

CARRIE. *(To JULIE)* Yes.

ERIC. And they respected each other. They were loyal to one another. Best friends, right?

JULIE. No, they weren't.

CARRIE. Yes. They were.

ERIC. Then why did they get divorced? Carrie? *(CARRIE doesn't respond. Beat.)* I'm just saying, if they were *loyal* to each other, if that's what brought them together, it sure was a *fleeting* loyalty wasn't it? And then what were they left with? Marriage is not friendship. It's a lot more than friendship.

JULIE. *(To OWEN)* I just want you to know that I'm really okay with all of this. The whole parent thing. At school I saw a therapist so I'm *fine*. I mean this doesn't bother me at all. I'm *fine*.

OWEN. Oh. *(Beat)* Great.

CARRIE. Or maybe it's not about friendship at all. Maybe all you need to have is a home gym and a lot of dinner parties. Right Eric?

ERIC. What're you getting at Carrie? That my parents don't really love each other, that they don't have a *real* love or something? Is that what you're implying Carrie?

CARRIE. I'm not *implying* anything.

ERIC. You're not?

CARRIE. No. I'm *saying* it, Eric.

OWEN. Wow. I am *hungry*.

ERIC. You're saying my parents don't really love each other? My parents who have been together for almost thirty years, who have sex every night, sometimes in the shower, who vacation in *Paris* for God's sakes, you're saying they don't love each other?

OWEN. Does anybody want something from the food car?

CARRIE. I think they *would* love each other, Eric. If they *knew how to.*

OWEN. Anybody?

JULIE. *(To Owen)* Yeah, maybe I'll have something-

ERIC. What does that mean? *(he laughs)* If they knew how to *love*?

CARRIE. *(Grabbing her sister as an exhibit)* I'm just *saying* Eric that maybe my parents couldn't love each other, maybe they weren't built for that, but they sure as hell love me and my sister. They would do anything for us. And I don't think that's a kind of love you understand because you've never experienced it.

JULIE. *(Subtly trying to shake free of CARRIE's grasp)* Or, you know what? Maybe I'll go with you—

ERIC. *I've never experienced it? Are you kidding?*

JULIE. Carrie, do you want chips or a water or something?

ERIC. Are you seriously saying that *my parents don't love me?* You're fucking insane. You're *nuts.*

CARRIE. If they love you so much how come they *never call you*?

ERIC. They *call* me….

CARRIE. Like once a year.

ERIC. They're *busy.*

CARRIE. *Obviously.*

OWEN. Come on, Julie, let's just go—

ERIC. This is—I can't even believe….

JULIE. Carrie?

(CARRIE doesn't respond. JULIE touches her shoulder.)

JULIE. I'll get you a water.

(JULIE and OWEN start to exit.)

CARRIE. No. *(Pause, JULIE stops.)* I want a coke.

(OWEN and JULIE exit. Pause.)

ERIC. So what about you?

CARRIE. What about me what? Haven't we already done me?

ERIC. No, you said I've never experienced this love, this *type* of love that you seem to think is so important, is like the *only* important type of love there is for you, the only one that leads to "successful" marriage and we've been together two years so I'm asking you, do you feel that type of love for me?

(Beat)

CARRIE. Eric…

ERIC. Don't dodge the question. Answer me.

CARRIE. I'm really upset right now and I don't think—

ERIC. So don't think! You shouldn't have to think about it! We're not *kids* anymore. We're not just sticking together until we *graduate*. I mean we're not just playing around here anymore. *(Beat)* Are we?

CARRIE. No. Of course we're not.

ERIC. So? *(Beat)* I mean, we're finding out all this stuff we never thought to ask before, some subtle, detailed stuff and surprise, we don't both believe it. We're not on the same page. We're not even in the same *love*. I mean: we don't even *love* each other the same way. And we both—the one thing we seem to agree about is that you *have to*. You have to love each other the same or else it *won't work*. So do we? Or I mean, could we? Or even: do we want to?

(A moment. CARRIE looks away from ERIC. Beat)

ERIC. *(Quieter)* Carrie… C'mon. *Tell* me.

(CARRIE looks at him. She is about to speak when OWEN and JULIE return with trays of food, laughing.)

OWEN. "Excuse me sir, can you please roast my nuts?"

(They laugh again. Before they can sit down, the train hits a bump

and JULIE is thrown back into OWEN. Her food flies all over him.)

JULIE. Oh my god—

(JULIE and OWEN collapse in laughter. They sit down, recovering from their laughter. Then they notice the uncomfortable silence between CARRIE and ERIC. An awkward pause.)

OWEN. This guy in the food car wanted his nuts roasted.

(OWEN and JULIE laugh again—a little. Pause.)

JULIE. *(To CARRIE)* I got you a coke. Carrie. I got you a coke. *(CARRIE doesn't react)* Do you want it or what?
    CARRIE. I don't know.
    JULIE. You *told* me to get you a coke.
    CARRIE. *(To ERIC)* I don't know.
    ERIC. What?
    CARRIE. I don't know if we could love each other the same way.
    JULIE. You guys are still talking about this?
    ERIC. You don't *know?*
    CARRIE. I mean, just now, you just... *(She looks at him.)* I mean what if something happens to me? And you're gone? You're out of there?
    ERIC. I didn't mean *me,* I wasn't talking about *myself*—
    OWEN. *(To JULIE, the following lines overlapping with Carrie and Eric's argument)* I lived for a while in Athens.
    CARRIE. Then who were you talking about?
    ERIC. I was—it was hypothetical. It was about people in general not ... it wasn't personal—
    JULIE. That's amazing! Italian is my favorite food.
    CARRIE. Really? When you said my parents never loved each other, that felt personal.
    OWEN. *(Noticing her error, but ignoring it)* No way. We should ... eat it together ... sometime.
    ERIC. Yeah well when you said my parents never loved *me,* you

know what Carrie?, that felt pretty damn personal too.

(OWEN bites into a chip. Everyone looks at him.)

OWEN. *(Offering to the group)* Chip?

(OWEN chews slowly, deliberately, making a funny face for Julie's benefit. She smiles at him.)

CARRIE. Right so, I mean, I'm sorry about that, I'm sorry I said that—
ERIC. Whatever.
CARRIE. No, I am, but… But I *meant* it. *(Beat)* I was talking about us. *(Beat)* And so were you. We were talking about, about what we can offer each other. About what we need. And I need a best friend.
ERIC. I *am* your friend, Carrie. You know that. I'm … you're my best friend.
CARRIE. Now. Now you are. But you just said, what you just said before, is that when that fades—
ERIC. *If* it fades, *if. I love you.* I am *in love* with you. And that's not gonna, there's nothing that says that that ever has to change.
CARRIE. But it might.
ERIC. But it *won't.*
CARRIE. It *might,* Eric. You might wake up one morning and just *notice* somebody else and think, well Carrie's not giving me what I need anymore, so…
ERIC. No. I wouldn't.
CARRIE. You said you would. That you'd be entitled to it. That your kids—*our* kids—would be *happier*—
ERIC. You're twisting my words around.
CARRIE. But… That's still ... the gist of it. Right?
ERIC. No. *(Weaker)* No.
CARRIE. That's not good enough for me. Or, that's not *enough* for me. I couldn't *believe* in us, Eric. *(Beat)* I don't *believe* in us now.

(Pause.)

ERIC. Huh.

JULIE. Okay, you guys have to stop. We're on a train. We're going to a wedding for god's sake. I mean, can you even hear yourselves? You guys love each other. I *know* you love each other. You've got, I mean, some people would *kill* for what you've got. You guys are *good*. You're good *together*.

CARRIE. *(To ERIC)* I *love* you, but I couldn't... I just don't...

JULIE. Carrie. *Stop it.*

ERIC. No Jules it's okay. I get it. *(To CARRIE)* You're right. We're not on the same page. You're already planning our demise, these horrible things, like getting cancer or not wanting to have sex with me and—And I mean, *(He laughs)* do I really want to be with somebody who's planning to withhold sex *twenty years* in advance? I don't think so.

JULIE. Eric...

ERIC. So yeah. You're right. There's nothing here. There is ... nothing here ... to believe in.

(ERIC stands and gets his bag.)

JULIE. Where are you going?

ERIC. I think I'm gonna *skip* the wedding actually, Jules.

JULIE. You don't have to—

ERIC. Yeah I do. I do. *(He gives JULIE a hug.)* You take care of yourself, okay? You're gonna be okay. You're gonna be fine, Jules. *(He shakes hands with OWEN.)* Nice meeting you man. Good luck out there.

OWEN. Yeah, you too.

CARRIE. You can't get out here. You don't even know where you are.

ERIC. Yeah that doesn't bother me. I'll figure it out.

(ERIC takes a step forward and then he stops. Somewhere toward the end of his speech the train comes to a stop.)

ERIC. *(To CARRIE)* You know ... the shitty part about this is ...

that no matter how bad things were gonna get, I mean *(He laughs.)* no matter how ugly you're gonna be … no matter how many *spots* you're gonna have … I'm always gonna remember you like this. Like how you are … right now. How we are … how we *were* right now. *(Beat)* And that's gonna be the worse part I think: tricking myself into believing that we really weren't that great together. Convincing myself it really wasn't going to work.

CARRIE. Eric…

ERIC. I gotta go. *(He kisses her forehead.)* I'm gonna go.

(ERIC exits. A pause and then CARRIE begins to cry. JULIE hugs her, also upset. Beat.

Carefully, OWEN takes JULIE's hand. She looks at him, surprised. They begin to smile at each other.

The train lurches forward.)

End of Play

PROPERTY PLOT

OWEN
Suitcase
Chips

JULIE
Suitcase
Makeup
Soda
Snack

CARRIE
Suitcase
Soda

ERIC
Suitcase

SET

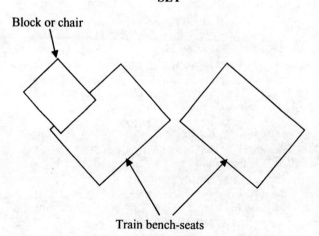

Block or chair

Train bench-seats

More Off-Off-Broadway Festival

FOURTH AND FIFTH SERIES
An Empty Space   Nothing Immediate   Open Admission
Batbrains   Me Too, Then!   "Hello, Ma!"

SIXTH SERIES
A Bench at the Edge   Seduction Duet

SEVENTH SERIES
MD 20/20   Passing Fancy

EIGHTH SERIES
Dreamboats   A Change from Routine   Auto-Erotic Misadventure

NINTH SERIES
Now Departing   Something to Eat   The Enchanted Mesa
The Dicks   Piece for an Audition

TENTH SERIES
Delta Triangle   Dispatches from Hell   Molly and James
Senior Prom   12:21 p.m.

ELEVENTH SERIES
Daddy's Home   Ghost Stories   Recensio   The Ties That Bind

TWELFTH SERIES
The Brannock Device   The Prettiest Girl in Lafayette
County   Slivovitz   Two and Twenty

THIRTEENTH SERIES
Beached   A Grave Encounter   No Problem   Reservations
for Two   Strawberry Preserves   What's a Girl to Do

FOURTEENTH SERIES
A Blind Date with Mary   Bums   Civilization and Its Mal-
contents   Do Over   Tradition 1A

FIFTEENTH SERIES
The Adventures of Captain Neato-Man   A Chance Meeting
Chateau Rene   Does This Woman Have a Name? ˙ For
Anne   The Heartbreak Tour   The Pledge

SIXTEENTH SERIES
As Angels Watch   Autumn Leaves   Goods   King of the
Pekinese Yellowtail   Uranium   Way Deep   The Whole
Truth   The Winning Number

SEVENTEENTH SERIES
Correct Address   Cowboys, Indians and Waitresses   Home-
bound   The Road to Nineveh   Your Life Is a Feature Film

EIGHTEENTH SERIES
How Many to Tango?   Just Thinking   Last Exit Before
Toll   Pasquini the Magnificent   Peace in Our Time   The
Power and the Glory   Something Rotten in Denmark   Vis-
iting Oliver

Plays from Samuel French

NINETEENTH SERIES
Awkward Silence   Cherry Blend with Vanilla   Family Names   Highwire   Nothing in Common   Pizza: A Love Story   The Spelling Bee

TWENTIETH SERIES
Pavane   The Art of Dating   Snow Stars   Life Comes to the Old Maid   The Appointment   A Winter Reunion

TWENTY-FIRST SERIES
Whoppers   Dolorosa Sanchez   At Land's End   In with Alma   With or Without You   Murmurs   Ballycastle

TWENTY-SECOND SERIES
Brothers   This Is How It Is   Because I Wanted to Say   Tremulous   The Last Dance   For Tiger Lilies Out of Season   The Most Perfect Day

TWENTY-THIRD SERIES
The Way to Miami   Harriet Tubman Visits a Therapist   Meridan, Mississippi   Studio Portrait   It's Okay, Honey   Francis Brick Needs No Introduction

TWENTY-FOURTH SERIES
The Last Cigarette   Flight of Fancy   Physical Therapy   Nothing in the World Like It   The Price You Pay   Pearls   Ophelia   A Significant Betrayal

TWENTY-FIFTH SERIES
Strawberry Fields   Sin Inch Adjustable   Evening Education   Hot Rot   A Pink Cadillac Nightmare   East of the Sun and West of the Moon

TWENTY-SIXTH SERIES
Tickets, Please!   Someplace Warm   The Test   A Closer Look   A Peace Replaced   Three Tables

TWENTY-SEVENTH SERIES
Born to be Blue   The Parrot   Flights   A Doctor's Visit   Three   Questions   The Davel's Parole

TWENTY-EIGTH SERIES
Leaving Tangier   Blueberry Waltz   Along for the Ride   A Low-Lying Fog   Quick and Dirty

TWENTY NINTH SERIES
Feet of Clay   All in Little Pieces   The King and the Condemned   Theodore Roosevelt Rotunda   The Casseroles of Far Rockaway   My Wife's Coat

THIRTIETH SERIES
Outside the Box   The Ex   The Sweet Room   Picture Perfecxt   Kerry and Angie   Defacing Michael Jackson